"Just please don't tell me that you're planning to try to fake out the guards by saying we slipped in here for a quick kiss," she muttered. "That's all I ask."

He undid his belt, unzipped his pants, and fell back on the sofa, taking her with him. She landed on top of him with a gasp of surprise and a splash of her long silky hair against his face.

"I wouldn't dream of it," he told her huskily. "We both know that a mere kiss wouldn't be nearly enough to convince anybody."

The scent of lilacs and springtime and something damn near close to heaven swirled around him, making his breath catch in his throat. Maybe . . . he . . . should rethink their strategy here, he decided, feeling his body begin to tighten. After all, this was only supposed to be a bit of make-believe for the benefit of the guards. This wasn't real . . . even if his body was having trouble telling the difference.

"This . . . isn't going to work," she said. "I mean, how stupid do you think these guys are?"

He grasped her waist and pulled her toward him. "Fo̶r̶ ̶̶ ̶̶," he whispered, "I hope t̶̶"

WHAT ARE *LOVESWEPT* ROMANCES?

They are stories of true romance and touching emotion. We believe those two very important ingredients are constants in our highly sensual and very believable stories in the LOVE-SWEPT line. Our goal is to give you, the reader, stories of consistently high quality that may sometimes make you laugh, sometimes make you cry, but are always fresh and creative and contain many delightful surprises within their pages.

Most romance fans read an enormous number of books. Those they truly love, they keep. Others may be traded with friends and soon forgotten. We hope that each LOVESWEPT romance will be a treasure—a "keeper." We will always try to publish

LOVE STORIES YOU'LL NEVER FORGET
BY AUTHORS YOU'LL ALWAYS REMEMBER

The Editors

Loveswept ®805

LICENSED TO SIN

FAYE HUGHES

BANTAM BOOKS

NEW YORK · TORONTO · LONDON · SYDNEY · AUCKLAND

This one is for my editor, Susan Brailey.

LICENSED TO SIN

A Bantam Book / September 1996

ISBN 0-553-44528-6

Published simultaneously in the United States and Canada

---

*Bantam Books are published by Bantam Books, a division of Bantam Dou-
bleday Dell Publishing Group, Inc. Its trademark, consisting of the words
"Bantam Books" and the portrayal of a rooster, is Registered in U.S. Patent
and Trademark Office and in other countries. Marca Registrada. Bantam
Books, 1540 Broadway, New York, New York 10036.*

PRINTED IN THE UNITED STATES OF AMERICA

OPM   0 9 8 7 6 5 4 3 2 1

ONE

She had the longest legs he'd ever seen.

A slow grin slid across Nick Benedict's face as he watched the brunette cocktail waitress make her way toward him through the crowded riverboat casino, a drink-laden tray held high above her head. Nice legs they were, too, he decided after a moment's reflection. Long and brown and perfectly curved, they were the kind of legs that could jump-start a dead man's heart and throw the concentration of a live one to hell and gone.

Nick took a swallow of his club soda and let his gaze move slowly up her body. The rest of her wasn't half bad, either.

She was a true *belleza*, a real beauty as his maternal grandfather would have said. She was in her late twenties, Nick guessed, probably only a few years younger than himself. She had lustrous dark hair that cascaded around her bare shoulders and a firm, tight body whose every delectable curve was hugged and accentuated by her costume, a skimpy little black and red thing that was somebody's idea of what a saloon girl might have worn on a nineteenth century paddle wheeler.

Not that he was one to quibble over little details like historical accuracy, Nick thought. His grin started to widen as she came even with the poker table and deposited a couple of drinks in front of the players. Especially since Nick liked the dress—or, rather, he liked the way the dress looked on her. In fact, when he filed his report on the *Vicksburg Lady* with his father, Nick intended to recommend that the costumer for Benedict Casinos' latest acquisition be given a substantial bonus for having come up with the idea for the staff's uniforms.

Nick sighed and gave his glass of club soda a gentle shake, clinking the melting ice cubes together.

Unfortunately, based on what he'd seen at the casino thus far, chances were excellent it would be the only positive thing in his report. Checking out the *Lady* was to have been his last official act before turning over the reins to his younger siblings. Nick had been hoping that he could conclude his business fairly quickly so that he could check out a piece of prime horse property just outside of Jackson that he had his heart set on buying.

Now it looked as if his meeting with the real estate agent would have to wait a while. There were problems at the *Vicksburg Lady*. Big problems. The kind associated with fixed card games, too-tight-to-be-believed slot machines, and weighted roulette wheels, the latter of which Nick had personal experience with since he'd lost five grand on one just a short time before in a futile attempt to disprove his own theories.

Of course, knowing there was a problem and coming up with a plan to rectify the situation were two completely different things. For starters, he wasn't sure how far up the management chain the cheating went. Until he knew, all he could do was investigate and pray that the Mississippi gaming commission didn't shut down the casino before he'd gotten to the bottom of things.

Taking another sip of his club soda, Nick returned his attention to the poker table. The game had been going for about thirty minutes, and the pot had grown progressively larger with each hand just like a Thanksgiving turkey being fattened up by a hungry pilgrim in anticipation of a feast. Only one player of the original four, a gray-haired man in his early sixties who'd already smoked his way through half a pack of cigarettes and looked ready to finish off the rest before the hour was through, remained in the game; the other three players had wisely folded and were sitting back in their respective chairs nursing wounded egos and watered-down drinks.

The gray-haired man had held his own up until now, but Nick knew the man didn't stand a chance of winning. Not while the dealer was dealing from a marked deck of cards. And certainly not with the cards the man had just been dealt: An ace and an eight, with what appeared to be two deuces and a three lying unturned on the table before him. A quick scan of the markings on the dealer's hand showed that he had a full house.

A neat trick, really, Nick thought coldly, since the man had dealt them off the bottom of the deck in full view of everyone at the table and the casino's surveillance team who were supposedly watching the feed from the security camera positioned less than three feet away.

A flash of red and black through Nick's peripheral vision captured his attention, and he turned in time to see the cocktail waitress walk to the other end of the poker table. He marveled again at the way she moved, with an economy of motion that didn't so much as ruffle a single feather of her dress's red boa trim. Several strands of her dark hair tumbled across her cheek as she leaned down to set her tray next to the gray-haired man, and Nick couldn't help but wonder if her hair felt as silkily soft to the touch as it looked—or if she looked as good out of the saloon girl getup as she did in it.

Nick felt his body start to tighten and took a deep breath, telling himself that he'd be better off concentrating on what was happening in the game rather than with staring at a beautiful woman he knew he didn't have the time to pursue.

He reluctantly began to turn away only to notice

her casting furtive glances out of the corner of her eye, looking first at the player's cards and then over at the dealer's hand. Her forehead wrinkled into a frown as though she'd noticed what the dealer was up to and was less than pleased by the discovery, then the frown faded and she slipped her hand into the side pocket of her uniform to retrieve a napkin.

"Here's your rum and coke, Mr. Pearce," she said, sliding the drink in front of the older man.

Her voice suited her, Nick decided with a smile. It was warm and throaty with just the softest twinge of a Southern drawl, a sound so undeniably seductive, it could probably steal away a man's soul with very little effort.

Pearce took another hit off his cigarette but didn't look up. "Rum? Hell, Jane, they must be working you too hard. I ordered a whiskey sour, the same drink I've ordered all night long."

Jane? Nick wondered, his smile deepening as he let his gaze slide over her curves one more time. Her voice may have suited her, but her name certainly did not. All the Janes he'd ever met were responsible, no-nonsense types who'd never inspire the kind of naughty little fantasies he was moments away from having about her.

"Sorry," Jane said sheepishly. She glanced at the balding blond-haired man sitting one chair over. "Then you must have been the one who ordered the rum?" she asked, sounding unsure.

Her smile was charming and ever so apologetic, but if Nick had been inclined to place a wager just then, he'd have put even money on the probability that she knew exactly what the man had ordered although why she was feigning confusion he couldn't say.

The blond-haired man grinned. "Guilty as charged, ma'am."

Pearce nodded at the dealer and tossed another chip onto the pile. "I'll raise another ten and then I call."

Jane picked up the rum and coke and leaned across the table in front of Pearce, skimming the paper napkin held in her other hand over his unturned cards the moment her body blocked the dealer's view. Then she straightened, slipped the napkin back into her pocket and transferred the whiskey sour from her tray to the table.

"Thanks, honey," Pearce said, and took a last hit off his cigarette which he then stubbed out in the already overflowing ashtray. He reached for his cards.

"Don't mention it," she practically purred.

Then with the trace of a sly, triumphant smile hovering around her mouth, she retrieved her tray and turned to go, leaving Nick to wonder why the hairs along the nape of his neck had suddenly begun to prickle.

Nick glanced back at the table and quickly scanned Pearce's cards. Gone were the markings so easily readable from before; instead, there were three new cards Nick couldn't identify although he had a funny feeling they would probably win Pearce the game.

What's more, Nick somehow didn't think Pearce was the one who'd changed them. For that matter, Nick doubted that Pearce had even been aware the dealer was cheating in the first place.

"Well, I'll be damned," Nick murmured in grudging admiration under his breath.

He now knew why Jane had pretended to screw up the drink orders. She'd needed an excuse to get close to Pearce's unturned cards, although her motive for intervening in the crooked card game was still unclear. Nick was fairly certain she didn't have a personal stake in the outcome of the game.

But intervene she had and with one of the slickest moves Nick had seen in his entire thirty-four years, which made him think that she was wasting her talents working as a cocktail waitress.

More important, though, it made him think that she might just be the one person who could tell him exactly what the hell was going on at the *Vicksburg Lady*. Provided, of course, that he was able to get to her before anyone else did.

Nick downed his drink and went after Jane as a whoop of excitement went up from the poker table behind him.

The way Nick saw it, once the dealer figured out what she'd just done—or, more likely, once the surveillance unit reviewed the feed from its video camera positioned above the poker table—the enigmatic brunette beauty with the longest legs he'd ever seen might find herself in more trouble than her altruistic act was worth.

Her partners were going to kill her . . . and just then, Jane Steele couldn't say she particularly blamed them.

Casting furtive glances over her shoulder to make sure she wasn't followed, she took the narrow metal stairs down to the casino's offices two rungs at a time. After all, she'd already made one incredibly stupid mistake that evening, the kind that could blow her assignment sky-high and possibly even cost Steele Angel Investigations a hefty retainer that the agency badly needed. Worse than that, it was the kind of mistake that had all the potential for getting her embroiled in a particularly nasty brand of trouble involving unamused bad guys, untraceable handguns, and a quick trip to a deserted spot along the river for a not-so-friendly chat.

Jane scowled and peered out the stairwell into the empty hallway. A security camera was mounted on the ceiling directly across from her, right above the unmarked door to the surveillance unit, but its lens was directed down the hall so her presence should still be undetected by the guards inside. Fortunately, her shift had ended so she wouldn't be expected back at the casino, but if she were caught hanging around a restricted area, she'd have some fast explaining to do.

She glanced at her watch. 7:29 P.M. She figured

she had about another minute or two before the guards took their evening break . . . provided, of course, they hadn't reviewed the video feed and seen what she'd done back at the poker table, in which case all bets were off.

"Damn," she muttered under her breath, then leaned against the wall to consider her options.

She supposed there was still a slim chance that she was worrying over nothing. From what she'd learned from her contact in casino security, the monitors in the surveillance room were programmed to change the origin of their feed source at intervals of every ten minutes unless a member of the unit decided to override. All of which meant that her activity at the poker table may not have been videotaped.

Jane closed her eyes for a moment. What the hell had she been thinking when she'd switched the three aces for Pearce's two deuces and a three? She was supposed to be the sensible one, for criminy's sake, the one who always prided herself on her ability to think things through before taking action. She was the one who kept her occasionally-less-than-logical partners in line by insisting that they play it strictly by the book, although this time she'd been the one who'd virtually thrown the book out the window.

So what if Will Pearce, a nice old man from Tallulah, Louisiana, who reminded her too damn much of her father, was getting himself fleeced in a crooked card game? It wasn't any of her business.

She was only there at *Benedict's Vicksburg Lady* to look for a runaway seventeen-year-old, not to try and fix the problems of a fool who ought to know better than to waste good money in a card game in the first place.

One of the metal stair rungs creaked above her. Jane froze. She glanced back up the stairs. Nothing. Not even a shadow out of place, yet the eerie feeling that there was someone up there, watching her every move, lingered.

She waited five seconds. Ten.

Still nothing.

Relax, she told herself forcefully, then raked her fingers through her hair and glanced back at the surveillance room. She was letting her imagination run away with her . . . or else she was feeling the first pangs of a well-earned guilty conscience for having jeopardized the assignment.

All she'd had to do was get the job as a cocktail waitress at the *Vicksburg Lady* and stake out the casino, the last place spoiled Jackson belle Marybeth Traynor had been spotted, and wait for her to return with her multitattooed and body-pierced boyfriend Seth, then call Daddy Traynor and let him do the rest. It was an easy assignment, really. Money in the bank, as her first cousin and partner John Angel would have said. But Jane had been opposed to taking the job right from the start. Mostly because she was the only one available—Johnny was still tied up doing surveillance of a possibly wayward wife, and Katherine, Jane's younger sister and second partner, was in Memphis doing an in-depth background check on a prospective employee for one of their corporate accounts.

Taking Traynor's job meant a sizable fee for the agency, but it also meant having to hang out in a casino for a couple of weeks, and Jane had seen enough of gamblers and gambling to last her a lifetime, thank you very much. Her father had been a professional gambler, playing cards in back-alley poker games and ritzy casinos with equal enthusiasm, going wherever he could find an open table and a group of people willing to play. He'd loved the game so much that he'd carted her and Kat all over the country, never staying put in one place long enough to grow roots, always searching for that one hand that would give him the big win.

Only the big win never happened.

What's more, her father had never quite accepted one of the fundamental rules of gambling: The odds were always in favor of the house.

Always.

The door to the surveillance unit slowly began to swing open.

But at least all of the games her father had played in had been fair, Jane reminded herself with a scowl, ducking back into the shadows of the stairwell. The *Vicksburg Lady* was cheating its customers—this despite the Benedict family's trademark assurance of always running an honest game, an assurance which was posted for all the world to see just above the riverboat's gangplank. True, not every game in the casino was rigged, but enough of them were to get them shut down by the gaming commission should they choose to investigate.

And Traynor case or not, Jane intended to do everything in her power to see that the commission did investigate and the *Vicksburg Lady* was permanently shut down . . . but first she had to retrieve that damn videotape—if it existed—before the dealer figured out what had happened and alerted his coconspirators.

Two burly-looking security guards, either certain to spot her should he decide to look in her direction, walked out into the hallway. Both were carrying a couple of medium-sized cardboard boxes and discussing the outcome of a football game from the previous day.

"It was pathetic, I tell you," the redhead said. "The Saints couldn't have scored a touchdown if they were the only friggin' team out on the field. Hell, my son's peewee squad could've kicked their butts."

"So why do you keep watching them if they're so damn bad?" his partner asked, grinning. "You into pain and humiliation, Fitzpatrick?"

Fitzpatrick shrugged. "Habit, I guess. Or maybe I just need something to bitch about . . . and that's one thing you can always count on the Saints to give you. Reason to bitch."

Both men laughed.

"You want to grab us some sodas while I drop these off in Tidwell's office?" Fitzpatrick asked.

"Sure."

His partner added his two boxes to the stack in Fitzpatrick's arms, then they turned and walked down the hallway in the opposite direction, continuing their gripe session about the New Orleans Saints.

Jane drew a sigh of relief and hurried over to the surveillance room. It seemed her luck was holding. If the guards had time to discuss football, the chances were excellent they hadn't seen the videotape from the poker table yet.

She glanced over her shoulder one last time to make sure she was alone, then reached into her pocket to retrieve a thin leather case from which she extracted a couple of metal lock picks. Once again, an eerie feeling that she was being watched swept over her, but she tried to shrug it off.

Nerves, she told herself. That and the fact that she really wasn't cut out for a life of crime.

She inserted the picks into the door's lock and gave them a deft flick of her wrist. Seconds later, the lock clicked and the door popped open. She slipped the picks back into their case and returned it to her pocket, then hurried into the security room lounge, easing the door closed behind her.

A nondescript brown plaid sofa and two matching easy chairs were positioned around the small room, along with a large two-way mirror next to a closed door. She crossed over to the door, opened it, and ducked inside the surveillance room.

The windowless unit was one of three on board

the *Vicksburg Lady* and much like she imagined was true with the others, it smelled of stale coffee and too many cigarettes. Two walls of monitors, twenty per wall with each showing black-and-white images of action from the casino, filled the room; a row of video recorders was positioned on a wire shelving unit next to the monitors.

Jane walked down the first set of monitors, scanning the descriptive labels attached to each. *Main Room, View 1. Main Room, View 2.* When she reached *View 11,* she found the monitor she was looking for although the image displayed on screen was of an adjacent blackjack table, rather than the poker game.

Jane traced the feed back to its recorder, then stopped the machine and pressed the eject button. One swift glance told her that it was a brand-new tape.

Feeling a queasiness start to form in the bottom of her stomach, she slipped the tape back into the recorder and reached for the next machine on the wire shelf. A scan of its tape confirmed what she had begun to suspect—namely, that all the tapes had been changed.

Unless Jane missed her guess, she now knew what Fitzpatrick was carrying in those cardboard boxes he was planning to drop off in the office of Robert Tidwell, the casino's newly appointed general manager.

"Damn!"

Jane jammed the second tape back into the machine, reset the record button, then backtracked out of the surveillance room as fast as her legs could carry her. She started to plot her next move, praying that Tidwell and his girlfriend, the acting head of casino security, were having a nice leisurely dinner somewhere and that he didn't decide to return to his office to watch a few videotapes—including Jane's small-screen debut, if, indeed, she'd made one—before she had a chance to get there.

"You've really screwed things up this time, Steele," she muttered under her breath, reaching for the doorknob to the hallway door. "What the hell are you planning to do for an encore?"

She yanked the door open and barreled her way straight into the broadest, firmest male chest she'd ever encountered in her entire thirty years.

She bit off a cry of alarm and started to topple over, but two large, strong hands encircled her waist and pulled her closer.

Her cheek brushed against the soft wool of his black sport coat, then came to rest against his black collarless silk shirt. The heat of his muscular body quickly seeped through the lightweight fabric, warming her skin straight down to her toes. She braced her hands against his chest and took a deep breath to restore her faltering equilibrium.

All she succeeded in doing, however, was overpowering her already overloaded senses with the scent of him . . . an exotic blend of spices and musk and all things gloriously, deliciously male that triggered almost every feminine response she had.

"Easy, *cara*," he murmured. "What's your hurry?"

His voice was low and deep, and it had a playful sexiness about it that sent her pulse rate soaring into the triple digits. It was the kind of voice that mamas always try to warn their daughters against listening to but never quite succeed. Worse, it was the kind of blatantly erotic, unquestionably male voice that could make an otherwise sensible, levelheaded woman start thinking about such crazy things as sultry jazz solos played late into the night and a pair of strong, muscular arms holding her tight on a dimly lit dance floor.

Jane slowly raised her head to meet his gaze. He looked as dangerous as he'd sounded, she decided, as in dark and virile and too damned handsome for his own good. He was tall, just over six feet, with jet-black hair combed straight back, laughing dark eyes, much too kissable lips, and an aura of sophisticated Latin charm that she suspected few women could resist.

He gave her a slow smile complete with a perfect set of dimples and a flash of even white teeth that could have made him a fortune advertising toothpaste, if he'd so desired.

But whatever it was this guy was selling, it sure as hell wasn't toothpaste, Jane thought, feeling herself flush. More likely than not, he was selling trouble. The kind of trouble she didn't need.

"Sorry," she said, pushing his hands off her

waist. "I guess I should start watching where I'm going."

"No problem, *cara*," he murmured again, taking a step back, though his amused gaze never wavered. "But you didn't answer my question . . . Why the big hurry?"

She reached behind her for the door handle and pulled it closed, almost half-convinced that he knew what she'd been up to.

Ridiculous, she told herself and raked her fingers through her hair, but he could pose a problem for her. She remembered having seen him upstairs in the casino—he was the kind of man it would be nearly impossible to forget. He'd been sipping a club soda and watching the poker game. She'd had him pegged as a professional gambler checking out the tables, although now . . .

Now she wasn't so sure.

"I'm sorry, Mr. . . . ?"

"Valdez," he answered smoothly. "Nick Valdez."

He gave her another smile, this one so warm it could have melted the chrome off a '57 Chevy.

He extended his hand. "And you are . . . ?"

"Jane Steele," she said.

This was crazy, she thought with growing confusion. She felt as though she were being hypnotized by his gaze, like some hapless rabbit caught in the headlights of an oncoming car.

Then his fingers slipped over hers. His touch was as incendiary as his smile had been. It sent shiver-inducing sparks racing up her hand and along her arm that seemed to energize every cell in her body before burning a path straight through to her soul.

Her mouth went dry. Her heart started to pound.

Forget the Chevy, she thought. If she wasn't careful, this man could very well cause a meltdown of every emotional defense she had . . . along with destroying whatever remained of her common sense.

She removed her hand from his grasp and crossed her arms against her chest.

"Were, ah, you aware, Mr. Valdez, that this area is restricted to casino employees?"

That toothpaste-perfect smile of his only seemed to grow wider.

"Actually, Janie, I believe this area of the riverboat is restricted for use by security personnel and casino administration employees. That means you shouldn't be down here, either."

"Ordinarily, you'd be right," she told him, refusing to be intimidated, "but not this time. I'm down here on official business."

And the sooner she hotfooted it on over to Tidwell's office to retrieve the videotape, the sooner she could conclude her "official business" too.

He took a step closer. "Well, my reason for being here is just as good, *cara.* I was looking for you."

"For me? Why?"

"Because I wanted to meet you," he said matter-of-factly. His gaze held hers for a long moment. "You see, I couldn't help noticing you back at the poker table a few minutes ago."

Once again his voice was filled with bad-boy charm and promises of forbidden pleasures. She took a deep breath and tried to tell herself that she was immune to its not-so-inconsiderable powers of seduction, that he didn't affect her at all, although she didn't quite believe her own reassurances. How could she when her body temperature was rising and her pulse rate already racing into the triple digits again?

"You brought Pearce luck," he went on. "A lot of it. The kind of luck I could have used about an hour ago at the roulette wheel when I dropped five grand."

She found herself smiling at him. "So let me guess . . . you decided to look for me because you think I'm some kind of good luck charm?"

He smiled back. "Some people believe in the power of a rabbit's foot, others a four-leaf clover. Why not a beautiful woman?"

He slowly ran the tip of his right index finger through the air near her bare shoulder, careful not to touch her but close enough to cause a light breeze to ruffle the feather boa trim of her uniform. Her stomach muscles began to tighten.

She sidestepped him and started to move slowly toward the stairwell.

"Sorry to disillusion you," she began.

"Then don't." Again with the twin-dimpled smile.

". . . but there's no such thing as magic charms," she said, feeling a rush of heat wash over her. "We make our own luck—good, bad, or in-between. Look, Mr. Valdez, I'm in something of a hurry—"

"Nick, please," he corrected. "And maybe you're right. Maybe we do make our own luck. But lately mine's been downright dismal. You could be just the thing to help me turn it around."

She stopped. "Oh? And how do you propose that I do that?"

"For starters, you could have dinner with me tonight . . . I know that would improve my luck immensely."

She laughed.

"Besides, we can talk," he said. "Get to know each other, have some fun . . . You do like to have fun, don't you, Janie?"

She felt herself flush again, straight through to the bone this time, and forced her gaze away. "The name is Jane."

"You're evading my question," he reminded her.

With good reason, too, she thought. Nick Valdez with his sexy eyes, high-voltage smile, and well-polished lines was the last person she needed to get herself entangled with. She knew exactly what kind of *fun* he was talking about having.

"I . . . don't . . . think that would be such a

good idea." She murmured, and glanced at her watch. "The casino has very strict rules against employees fraternizing with customers." She had even stricter rules against getting involved with men like him.

"Now, if you'll excuse me," she said, "I really do need to go."

She headed toward the stairwell.

"I'm sorry to hear you feel that way, *cara*," he said "It would have made everything so much easier if you'd only said yes."

His voice had lost its smooth-as-silk edge. It was cold and impersonal, and it stopped her dead in her tracks.

She turned back.

"Made what easier?" she asked, feeling a chill slide down her spine.

He met her gaze. "Having our little discussion . . . you see, I saw you switch Pearce's cards back at the poker table."

He gave her another smile. Even his dimples seemed to hold a chill.

"Now all I need to know," he said, "is what you intend to do to persuade me not to report you to the gaming commission."

TWO

A few seconds ticked by.

Nick wasn't sure what he was expecting Jane to do—blush a guilty shade of red to match the feather boa trim of her uniform, then break down and confess right there on the spot, or maybe go totally ballistic on him, slamming him up against the wall and glaring at him with those calm sea-green eyes of hers turning as stormy as the ocean in the middle of a typhoon. As it was, she did neither.

In fact, she didn't seem to react to his threat at all. At least not visibly.

"Tell me, Mr. Valdez," she murmured, taking a step toward him.

Her voice was cool and controlled and perfectly modulated, yet his heart started to pound and his body grew to full arousal—mostly because her soft Southern drawl was the smoke-tinged contralto of every erotic fantasy he'd ever had, a sound so starkly, so unquestionably sensuous, it had the power to set his libidinous imagination positively ablaze like a lit match to a slip of paper.

"Do you have much success with this back-street seduction routine of yours?" she went on. "Blackmailing women with all kinds of trumped-up accusations in a pitiful attempt to get them to go out with you?"

She came to a stop and stared up at him. A soft whisper of her perfume, some kind of surprisingly erotic combination of lilacs and springtime, wafted around him, making it hard for him to stay focused on anything but smiling at her.

"Trust me, *cara*," he murmured back. "I've never had to resort to blackmailing a woman in order to get a date . . . and my accusation about your cheating at the poker table tonight isn't a trumped-up charge. I saw the game, remember? And I saw you switch Pearce's cards when you served his drink."

"Then why didn't you report me to the dealer when you thought it happened?"

"I think you know the answer to that one."

She made no response, not even so much as an involuntary flutter of an eyelash.

He smiled again. Even without that sleight of hand magic she'd demonstrated upstairs, something told him that she'd make one hell of a poker player.

"The dealer would be the last person I'd ever tell, because the game was rigged," he added, deciding to lay out most of his cards on the table in the hope that she'd feel compelled to do the same.

Still he got no response from her.

"The dealer was using a marked deck, Janie," he went on patiently. "Pearce was being set up to take a fall, just like I'd been set up at the roulette table a little earlier. Since the security cameras were trained on both games and no one from the casino's surveillance unit ever showed up to put a stop to it, I'm guessing that the management here at the *Vicksburg Lady* approves of swindling its patrons. I'm also guessing that you don't particularly care for their policy, which is why you switched Pearce's cards."

She regarded him for a long moment, her expression impossible to read. "If you believe you've been cheated by the casino, Mr. Valdez, I suggest you file that complaint with the gaming commission as you'd threatened to do a few minutes ago."

"Yeah, I could do that, but it wouldn't get me my five grand back."

"And neither can I."

"No?" he asked, reaching for her hand.

The feel of her was electric. It sizzled his skin, fired his blood, and made the act of breathing become one of the most difficult tasks he'd ever had to perform.

His gaze locked with hers. He watched the flicker of sexual awareness flash across her face, felt her quick intake of breath, and knew that she was feeling the same way about him that he was about her.

"I, ah, was kind of hoping that you could help me out," he said huskily, sliding his thumb along her palm in a lazy circle. "Like the way you helped out your pal Pearce tonight."

He'd been wrong about her eyes, he decided. Rather than reminding him of some storm-tossed sea when she dropped her cool facade, they'd deepened in color to the lush and verdant green of a gently rolling Mississippi hillside, a color brimming with life and passion, a color he didn't think he could ever get enough of.

Her lips opened slightly, and he found himself fantasizing about slowly sliding his hand down her arm to encircle her waist . . . about pulling her body close enough to his for him to feel every one of her soft, luscious curves pressed intimately against him . . . about the throaty murmurs of feminine satisfaction that she'd make when he kissed her good and long and hard.

His mouth went as dry as a Nevada summer. His body grew tighter, almost to the point of causing him pain.

Damn, he thought. Maybe this wasn't such a great idea. Instead of grilling her for information about the rigged games on board the *Vicksburg Lady*, all he seemed to be doing was indulging his libido, a pleasant enough pastime except that he couldn't afford to be seduced by a soft smile and a killer pair of legs just then . . . not when he knew that the emotional price tag would likely be a hefty one—and especially not when the reputation of Benedict Casinos was hanging in the balance.

He took a slow, deep breath and tried to refocus, but it did little to lessen his sudden aching want for her. He had a feeling that nothing ever would.

As though she'd read the direction his thoughts had headed, a flush crept over her cheeks. She slipped her hand out of his grasp and took a step back.

"I don't think we should . . . oh, this is absurd," she said, sounding as out of emotional control as he felt himself. "Will Pearce is not my *pal*, and I didn't switch his cards."

"Why don't I believe you?"

"Because you don't want to accept the truth," she said, looking him square in the eye.

Her gaze was steady and her stance filled with what appeared to be an unshakable confidence, which was exactly how a high roller would respond to an opponent in a poker game when he was tapped out, his hand had just been called, and all he held was a pair of deuces.

She was good. *Damn good.*

"You lost big tonight," she went on. "Your ego can't handle it, so you manufactured this little fantasy about the casino's games being rigged . . . and about my slipping Mr. Pearce three aces."

His smile deepened. "Nice bluff, *cara*, only you left the table before Pearce played his hand . . .

and I never said which cards I thought you'd slipped him."

Footfalls sounded down the hallway. Nick glanced over his shoulder in time to see the two burly-looking security guards heading straight toward them.

"It appears we've got company," he murmured. "Why don't we find some quiet little spot in the casino's lounge to continue our conversation?"

He turned back to face her but the only response he received was the clatter of her high heels on the metal rungs of the staircase as she raced back upstairs.

Nick sighed and watched her go, vowing that he'd catch up with her later . . . and that they'd finish their little chat whether she wanted to or not. For now, he had other things to worry about, such as finding out just how deeply imbedded in the management structure the *Vicksburg Lady*'s problems were.

"You lost, buddy?" asked one of the guards.

"More like momentarily led astray."

"Say what?"

Nick turned and gave the two men a smile. "Nothing," he said. Then he glanced at his watch. "You know, I'm glad I ran into you guys. My name is Nick Valdez. I've got an appointment with Robert Tidwell to discuss setting up an account. Maybe you can point me in the direction of his office?"

❖————————❖

"Nice bluff, cara, *only you left the table before Pearce played his hand . . ."*

Jane scowled and dropped the leather case containing her lock picks back into her uniform pocket, then slipped inside Robert Tidwell's office, closing the door behind her with more noise than was probably advisable under the circumstances.

Dammit, but she seemed to be setting some kind of record for making potentially costly blunders. First, she'd forgotten her primary objective, the one Steele Angel Investigations had been hired to perform—namely, getting herself a temporary post at the casino and waiting for the missing Marybeth Traynor to reappear. Next, she'd allowed her sense of fair play to cause her to interfere in the outcome of a crooked card game, even when it meant running the risk of blowing her cover. Then, she'd made her biggest mistake of all. She'd nearly confessed everything to a sexy-eyed Latin charmer who acted as though the Good Lord himself had given him a license to sin.

Feeling herself blush, Jane crossed over to the neat row of cardboard boxes of videotapes stored on the oak credenza next to the windowless wall.

No doubt about it, Nick Valdez was trouble, but assessing the actual level of danger that he posed to her safety was tricky. She didn't believe for a moment that he would follow through on his threat to report her to the gaming commission—ditto to any of the casino management. It didn't seem to be his style. She also didn't think that he was serious when he'd asked for her help in getting his money back. A professional gambler wouldn't need her help or anyone else's in outwitting a none-too-clever dealer running a crooked table. Men who made their living with cards knew every underhanded trick there was to know about playing the game. His request had been more like some kind of a test, which made her nervous.

It also made her think that she should probably run as far and as fast as she could in the opposite direction should she ever see him again . . . primarily because he seemed to wreak absolute havoc with her equilibrium with a minimum of effort on his part.

She could still feel the heat of his dimpled smile warming her straight through to her core, melting bones along with common sense. What's worse, she could still feel the touch of his hand against her palm, how it made her feel things she never even thought herself capable of feeling . . . made her want something she couldn't even put into words.

Jane muttered a curse under her breath and reached for the first box. Maybe she was having some kind of premature midlife crisis or something, she thought, sorting through the videotapes. Or maybe her desire to shut down *Benedict's Vicksburg Lady* was simply overshadowing everything else, including her ability to think straight.

She closed the box and reached for the next one, trying to work as quickly as she could. She wasn't sure how much time she had to find the tape before

Tidwell returned. For that matter, she didn't even know if he would be returning to his office that night at all.

In the twenty-four hours she'd been on board the riverboat, Tidwell's schedule had been impossible to pin down. From what she'd managed to pick up from her source in security—a personable enough young man who'd made no secret of his dislike for Tidwell's recent appointment of his girlfriend, Barbara Weems, to the position of acting chief of security—the casino manager spent more time down at the *Vicksburg Lady* in the evenings than he did during normal work hours.

Jane reached for the third box. She flipped open the lid and began to sort through the tapes. When she came across the one marked *Main Room, View 11*, she felt a wave of relief wash over her.

"Finally."

She tucked the tape under her arm, flipped the lid to the box closed, and turned toward the door. Then she heard it. The low murmur of voices. Male voices, to be precise, including one that sounded like the sexy tones of Nick Valdez, although she told herself she was probably just imagining that part.

At any rate, the voices were coming from outside in the hall . . . and they were quickly followed by the scrape of a key being inserted into the door's lock.

Tidwell had returned, she thought, feeling her heart jump into her throat. Possibly with a guard. Maybe even two.

"Damn!"

Jane quickly glanced around her, looking from the credenza, past Tidwell's neat-as-a-pin desk, and over to his built-in, floor-to-ceiling wet bar with its sliding rattan doors. There were no exits and damn few places for her to hide. She glanced back at the door just as the lock clicked open.

She had no intention of standing there until Tidwell caught her, like some meek little lamb awaiting the proverbial slaughter, either.

She muttered another curse under her breath. Why couldn't one damn thing she did go right that night? Just one?

She bolted for the wet bar.

"So how have you been enjoying your visit to *Benedict's Vicksburg Lady* thus far, Mr. Valdez?"

Robert Tidwell was a tall, sandy-haired man in his early forties with the oily smile and all the smarmy charm of a used car salesman hoping to unload a lemon on an unsuspecting customer.

Nick leaned back in his overstuffed wing chair and returned the smile, wishing that he could simply kick Tidwell out of the casino right then and there and be done with the whole damned thing.

Unfortunately, identifying the man as a sleaze and proving that he was behind the rigged games at the *Vicksburg Lady* were two entirely different things. Nick figured he would need proof—and incontrovertible proof at that—before taking action.

He also figured that the best way, maybe the only way, of getting that proof was to have Tidwell provide it himself, which was why Nick had decided to set himself up as bait.

The plan was simple enough, and orchestrating the groundwork for the sting deceptively easy. A few telephone calls had arranged his cover as a bored financier from Las Vegas with a weakness for poker and high living. A request for a private game from Tidwell would do the rest . . . because if Tidwell was participating in the fleecing of the *Lady*'s patrons, as Nick suspected was the case, the casino manager wouldn't be able to resist the temptation of setting up a crooked card game for a high roller with money to burn.

"Enjoying myself?" Nick asked with a lazy drawl. "Well, that all depends on how you define the term, I guess. I didn't like losing at roulette tonight, but then poker's always been more of my game."

Tidwell opened a silver-plated rectangular box on his desk and offered Nick a cigar, which he refused, then selected one for himself.

"Maybe your luck will improve when you switch to cards," Tidwell said, clipping off the end of his cigar.

"I'm counting on it," Nick said. *Just as I'm counting on your luck running out.*

Nick crossed his legs. "But I do like the casino's nineteenth century ambience," he went on. "I think it all works beautifully . . . the decor, the design of the tables themselves, even the period-inspired uniforms your staff wears."

A faint trace of lilacs, probably more memory than anything else, wafted around him then, as gentle and soft as a kiss.

He smiled again. At least the staff's choice in working attire *really* worked for him. Especially the way a certain brunette wore hers, he thought, feeling his attention begin to drift back to the oh-so-delectable Ms. Steele with her long, long legs, coolly vibrant sea-green eyes, and lustrous dark hair . . . hair that he could easily imagine himself running his hands through when he kissed her, each strand sliding over his fingers like spun silk.

He had been imagining himself kissing her, too . . . imagining the soft crush of her full, rounded breasts against his chest . . . wondering about the taste of her mouth beneath his, if it would be sweet enough to warm his heart or hot enough to scorch his soul . . . speculating about the feel of her tongue as it did a slow, erotic tango with his.

Tidwell struck a match and lit his cigar. "Benedicts spared little expense in refurbishing the *Lady*," he said, exhaling a thin ribbon of smoke. "In fact, some of the antiques . . ."

Nick took a deep breath, trying to refocus, as Tidwell rambled on about the antiques strewn throughout the casino. Nick knew he shouldn't be fantasizing about kissing Jane. Not now at any rate. He should be concentrating on the conversation—hell, it was vital that he pay careful attention to everything Tidwell said—but he couldn't seem to switch mental gears back to Tidwell, no matter how hard he tried.

Nick hadn't been able to stop thinking about Jane since the moment he'd seen her walking across the casino. He couldn't stop playing the memory of their brief conversation in front of the surveillance room over and over in his mind, specifically the part where he'd held her hand. It had been like touching fire.

He'd felt the heat all the way down to the soles of his feet . . . still felt the heat, in fact.

Just as he could still smell the scent of her perfume, still feel it spinning his imagination even further out of control.

Jesus, he thought, closing his eyes for a moment to regain his composure. What the hell was the matter with him? He'd just met the woman. He didn't know a damn thing about her.

All he knew was she was a slick enough card cheat to switch three marked cards in front of a roomful of people and not be spotted by the dealer, then break into a locked room to retrieve the videotape of her sleight of hand magic trick without leaving any telltale traces behind of her visit . . . both of which meant that she was no ordinary cocktail waitress. Just what she was other than a potentially dangerous distraction, he couldn't really say . . . but he sure as hell intended to find out.

Nick opened his eyes and forced his attention back to the casino manager.

". . . be happy to set up an account for you, Mr. Valdez," Tidwell was saying.

Nick took another slow, deep breath. "That's, ah, great."

Tidwell smiled again. "We hope you'll stay at the hotel as our guest. I've taken the liberty of making the necessary changes to your accommodations so there'll be no charge for your visit."

"Thank you."

Because of a quirk in Mississippi law, gambling was not permitted onshore, although the restriction was bound to be lifted soon, thanks to a flurry of new bills presented to the state legislature nearly every session. Until then, the *Vicksburg Lady*, along with several other riverboat casinos, was permanently docked along the shoreline of the Mississippi River. The Benedict Inn, less than two hundred feet away from the dock, was a small, tastefully decorated hotel that carried through its nineteenth century riverboat theme.

"Our pleasure," Tidwell said. "And if there's anything else we can do to make your visit more pleasant here in Vicksburg—arrange for a dinner companion one evening, perhaps?—just ask."

Nick shifted his position in his chair. As cues went, Tidwell's offer was near perfect.

"Thanks but I prefer to choose my own dates," Nick said. "But there is one thing you could do for me . . . I'd like to play some poker while I'm here."

"We have several tables on board the *Lady*. I

could make arrangements to have you sit in on the next game, if you'd like."

Nick laughed. "That's not really what I had in mind. I was hoping for something more challenging, with higher stakes . . . if you know what I mean."

Tidwell took another draw on his cigar, regarding Nick for a long moment through the swirl of smoke.

"You want me to set up a private game for you?" Tidwell asked.

"Yes."

Something flitted through Nick's peripheral vision then. It was some kind of movement from the far left side of the room, just out of Tidwell's line of sight. A flash of color mostly. Red.

Nick glanced toward the wet bar. It was a built-in that ran from the floor to the ceiling, the kind that had a minirefrigerator on the bottom, several cupboards on the top and just enough counter space in the middle to mix cocktails. For the briefest of seconds, Nick thought that he saw someone peering at him through the slats of its sliding rattan doors.

Ridiculous, he told himself.

Then it—whatever it was—moved again behind the slats. Only this time part of that something slipped through one of the door's narrow strips of rattan and floated down to the carpeting.

Nick squinted. From where he sat, it looked suspiciously like a small red feather . . . just the sort that might be used on the trim of a certain brunette cocktail waitress's uniform.

Well, I'll be damned.

Nick grinned, now knowing why he'd been haunted by the faint scent of Jane's perfume ever since he'd walked into the room. More than that, he also knew where Jane had been rushing off to in such a hurry when she'd left him back in front of the surveillance room. What he didn't know was what she was looking for in Tidwell's office and how she'd ended up hiding in the wet bar.

Tidwell flicked ash toward the marble tray on his desk and stood.

"I think a private game could be arranged for you, Mr. Valdez," he murmured, turning toward the bar. "Why don't I fix us a drink and we can discuss it."

Jane decided that now might be a good time to start panicking.

She glanced from side to side, careful not to jostle any of the glassware lining the rear of the countertop, looking for a weapon of some kind that she could use to defend herself. Only there weren't any unless she counted the videotape she still held in her hand or the highball glasses stored behind her, and she doubted if either would do her much good even if she started flinging them at Tidwell the moment he opened the cabinet doors.

Too bad she didn't share her sister's passion for

kickboxing, Jane thought dryly, or her cousin Johnny's gift for talking his way out of anything. At least then she might have stood an even chance of extricating herself from this mess.

"I'd just as soon we pass on the drinks for now," Nick said.

Tidwell came to a stop less than three feet away from the wet bar. He took another puff of his cigar and glanced back at Nick.

Jane waited, too afraid to breathe for fear Tidwell might hear her.

Then he shrugged. "Suit yourself." He returned to his desk.

Jane released her held breath, thanking the powers that be for her reprieve, even if it was only a temporary one. She closed her eyes and rested her chin on her pulled-up knees, promising herself that if she got out of this relatively unscathed, she'd listen to the advice she'd been dispensing to Kat and Johnny for years and never do anything so incredibly stupid as try and reinvent the rule book again.

"What I have in mind is just a friendly game of poker," she heard Nick say. "Something along the lines of a progressive pot, no limits on bets . . . and with you acting as the dealer."

At least she had small comfort in knowing that she wasn't the only one prone to behaving in an incredibly stupid fashion. She opened her eyes and raised her head. Had Nick completely lost his mind? she wondered with a frown. Why on earth would he ask Tidwell to set up a card game when he believed the casino had already ripped him off for five grand?

That queasy feeling she'd had earlier in the pit of her stomach returned, only stronger this time, because it suddenly occurred to her that Nick may have been planning to try and turn the tables on Tidwell by duplicating her three-aces-for-two-deuces-and-a-three trick in an attempt to win back his lost money. If so, he'd never make it off the riverboat.

Not alive at any rate.

"Like I said before," Tidwell murmured, "I can arrange a game for you."

She heard him flip through the pages of what she assumed to be an appointment calendar. "Tell me . . . how long are you planning to stay in Vicksburg, Mr. Valdez?"

A tap sounded on the office door before Nick could answer.

Jane peered through the slats of the rattan door and watched an overly made-up blond in her midforties, whom Jane deduced to be Barbara Weems, stick her head into the room.

"Robert?" Barbara then nodded toward the hallway, indicating that he should follow her.

"Excuse me," Tidwell said. "Casino business. It should only take a minute."

"No problem," Nick said, sounding as though he didn't have a care in the world. He reached for the long silver box on Tidwell's desk and withdrew a cigar, then leaned back in his chair to contemplate it.

With his own cigar clamped between his teeth, Tidwell skirted his desk and followed Barbara out into the hallway, closing the door firmly behind him.

That's when Nick sprang to his feet with pantherlike grace. Slipping the unlit cigar into his jacket pocket, he crossed over to the wet bar and slid open its rattan doors before Jane could do much more than gape up at him in surprise.

"I think you're a little too old to be playing hide-and-seek, *cara*," he said softly.

"I—"

He slid his hands around her waist, sending dozens of electrifying tingles shimmering down her spine. Then he pulled her toward him until her legs swung off the counter and dropped to the carpeting. She leaned against him for a moment until she regained her balance.

Big mistake.

The heat of his body swept over her with the force of a tsunami, laying waste to her equilibrium the way the wave would a tiny fishing village caught in its path of destruction.

Their gazes locked. Her heart started to pound. She felt as though her knees would buckle at any moment.

"Or are you playing a different kind of game tonight?" he asked in a husky-tinged whisper that made her want to shiver. "A decidedly *dangerous* game?"

"This isn't a game."

But what they were doing was dangerous, she decided. Extremely so. Although which posed the biggest threat just then—getting caught by Tidwell, who was only on the other side of the door, or standing there with Nick's arms around her waist, staring into his laughing dark eyes, feeling a need for him that shook her to her very core—Jane couldn't say.

He slowly released her and reached for the videocassette in her hand.

"Main Room, View Eleven?" He turned the tape over in his hand. "Now why do I think this isn't a copy of the latest blockbuster that you picked up from the corner video store?"

"Give that back!"

She made a grab for the cassette, but he held it out of reach.

"Not so loud," he cautioned, nodding toward the door. "We wouldn't want our friends to join us just yet, now would we?"

The low murmur of Tidwell's voice filtered back into the room, and Jane clamped her mouth shut. She took a deep breath and tried again, speaking softer this time.

"May I have the tape back? Please?"

"What's on it?"

"I—I'm not sure." Which was precisely the truth.

He studied her for a moment, then glanced at the cassette. "It looks like it's one of the casino's surveillance tapes. Hmm, I wonder . . . would *View Eleven* be anywhere near the poker table where Will Pearce was playing tonight?"

She considered lying but knew it would only be an exercise in futility. So she nodded.

Nick smiled, dazzling her with a double shot of dimples. "You did switch his cards, didn't you, Janie?"

She took a deep breath. "Yes, I switched his cards and, yes, the deck was marked like you said. Now will you give me the damned tape so I can get out of here before Tidwell catches me?"

"You can't go anywhere just now, *cara*, because Tidwell is still outside in the hall. However, I will help you out of this little jam you've gotten yourself in provided you return the favor and help me."

She eyed him suspiciously. "What do you want?"

"Information for starters. Anything you can tell me on how they're rigging the games . . . who's involved . . . how deep the corruption goes. That sort of thing. I'm scheduling a friendly little game with Tidwell to recoup my five grand and want to be as prepared as I possibly can for any shenanigans."

She scowled at him. "You can't be serious! Do you honestly think that you can cheat your way out of a rigged game?"

"You did," he reminded her with a grin.

"Yeah, but you busted me. And Tidwell will too if he sees this tape."

She reached for the cassette, but he again held it just out of her reach.

"Not so fast," he said. "I think I like having a bargaining chip where you're concerned. Maybe I'll hold on to this for a while."

Then he slid the cassette into the rear waistband of his pants.

"I'm staying at the Benedict Inn," he went on. "Room four-twelve. Why don't you meet me there in an hour? That'll give me time to conclude my business with Tidwell, and it should give you more than enough time to get out of here unnoticed."

She stared at him for a moment. "This isn't a game, Nick," she told him again.

She spoke slowly, enunciating her words with care this time, wanting to be certain that he fully understood the gravity of the situation they were in. "This is serious," she went on. "Deadly serious. You don't know what you're getting yourself involved in."

His gaze locked with hers again.

"The trouble is I think I do know, *cara* . . . but I still can't seem to help myself."

Then he leaned down and slid his lips over hers. It was a kiss as soft as the brush of angels' wings . . . and as hot as the caress of a demon. It was a simple kiss, only a gentle skimming of lips over lips for the briefest of seconds, yet its impact was considerable. She felt swamped by emotion, completely engulfed by an impossible-to-cool fever for his touch.

It scared her even more than the absolute lunacy he was proposing to do in the card game.

He pulled back and gave her a smile. "One hour," he said, turning to go. "Room four-twelve."

Then he opened the door and walked out into the hallway to distract Tidwell . . . while she tried vainly to pretend that she hadn't been rocked to her very foundation by what amounted to little more than a quick peck on the lips from a virtual stranger.

"Sweet heaven," she whispered, and closed her eyes.

Her father had always told her that God kept watch over fools and drunkards. She hoped her father was right.

She was feeling ridiculously a little like both.

THREE

When Nick arrived at his hotel room an hour and fifteen minutes later, Jane was nowhere to be seen. Deciding that he'd been stood up—or else she'd gotten tired of waiting for him to get there and had simply left—he muttered a curse and fished in his coat pocket for his room key. He inserted it into the lock and opened the door.

"You're late."

Her smoke-tinged contralto seemed to wrap itself around him like an embrace, stealing his breath for a moment and bringing him to a complete stop.

He glanced around the room, almost afraid his imagination was working overtime again, conjuring up auditory hallucinations of Jane to accompany the haunting mental images of her long legs and erotic sensuality that he'd been plagued with since the moment they'd met . . . mental images that had only been strengthened by that brief, coronary-inducing kiss they'd shared in Tidwell's office when Nick's shaky grip on his self-control had begun to slip.

This was no hallucination.

Jane sat at the table near the window, looking as delectable as ever, although he got the feeling that she was more than a little annoyed with him. She was bundled up in a heavy gray coat; her arms were folded sternly over her chest and her long brown legs primly crossed at the thigh.

Even so, his pulse began to race. One look at her was enough to make him feel like a bumbling adolescent alone with a girl for the first time.

He took a deep breath, then slowly exhaled, and gave her a grin. "One of these days you're going to have to show me how you do that," he said, taking off his coat. He dropped it on the bed and walked toward her. "Open locked doors without keys, I mean."

She slowly stood up, but didn't uncross her arms. "Can I have my tape back, please?"

"Funny, I thought the tape belonged to the *Vicksburg Lady*," he teased.

She met his gaze head-on. "And I thought that we had a deal."

A few seconds passed.

"We do," he said quietly, motioning for her to sit back down. "And I'll keep my end of the bargain . . . provided that you keep yours."

It was a lie, of course, and one that he wasn't particularly proud of telling. If the videocassette contained footage of the crooked card game as they suspected it did, he had no intention of ever surrendering it. Evidence of the problems on board the *Lady* was too damned hard to come by.

Of course, he knew that if he leveled with Jane, if he explained why he needed the tape, she'd probably understand. Unfortunately, the point was moot. He couldn't tell her when he hadn't decided if he could trust her.

And how could he trust her when he still wasn't sure what she was up to?

"As I recall," he said, taking the chair across from hers, "part of the deal we struck when I pulled you from the wet bar involved your sharing everything that you know about what's going on around here. Why don't we start by your telling me who you really are?"

She gave him a puzzled frown. "But you already know who I am. I'm Jane Steele."

"Uh-huh. And who, exactly, is Jane Steele?"

He crossed his legs and linked his fingers over his knee, then gave her another smile.

"And don't tell me she's a cocktail waitress from Vicksburg, Mississippi," he went on. "Remember, I've seen the way you switched those cards. That's not exactly a skill the casino teaches you along with serving drink orders."

She regarded him for a moment longer, shrugged off her coat and tossed it across the arm of her chair, and sat back down. She was still wearing her uniform. Its hem began to slide up along her thigh, giving him another glimpse of its perfectly proportioned curves.

His body began to tighten, grow hard. He swallowed and averted his gaze for a moment, although it didn't seem to help.

"I can also shuffle a deck using only one hand," she said dryly. "And I can deal the cards in descending or ascending order by their suits if I wanted to. So what? It's nothing more than parlor tricks that I learned from my father."

"Your father?" He glanced back at her. "And who might he be?"

"No one you'd likely have ever heard of," she told him. "But he used to be a professional card player."

"Used to be? Meaning he's retired?"

Her gaze didn't waver. "Meaning the game eventually killed him . . . just the way it'll kill anyone if he's fool enough to stay in it too long."

Bitterness colored her voice. It was the kind of rancor that can eat away at a person's soul if one doesn't find a way to eradicate it.

"The doctors said it was a bad heart," she went on, glancing down at the carpet. "They told him to take it easy, to watch his diet . . . give up the cards. Cutting out the extra salt and learning to exercise was the easy part, but giving up the game . . ."

She sighed and raked a hand through her hair. "The thing is, he couldn't have stopped even if he'd wanted to. Compulsive gambling . . . it's a disease, Nick. It's as devastating as drug addiction, only there's not a damn thing anyone can do to stop it because it's all perfectly legal. That means the pushers—the casinos like the *Vicksburg Lady* and all the others that people like the Benedict family operate—they don't have to worry about doing jail time for their crimes, while people like my father only end up losing it all."

He felt something tighten inside him. "I'm sorry," he said softly. "But he was a grown man, *cara*. He knew the risks when he sat down at the table."

"Yeah, he knew the risks. He even knew the odds were always going to be in favor of the house, but he ignored them . . . just like every other gambler does when he walks through the doors of a casino to place a bet. Besides, I told you he was addicted to the game. Nothing else mattered to him except the cards. Hell, when I was ten years old, he even put me and my younger sister up as collateral to hold his spot in a private game in Las Vegas while he ran back to our hotel room to get more money."

Anger snaked through him, anger that a parent could be so self-indulgent as to let a damned game endanger the emotional well-being of a child . . . anger that too many of Jane's accusations about the gambling industry were right on target, much as Nick hated to admit it.

It was a dirty business. He knew that better than anyone, but he was happy to say that his family had always tried their level best to keep it clean. Still, after having spent the first thirty-four years of his life living in the glitz and tarnished glamour of a casino—and after having had a marriage fall victim to its demanding lifestyle three years earlier—he'd finally decided that he needed a change. Something where fresh air rather than stale smoke was the norm. Where the only time people ever tried to figure out the angles was when they were planning to build something.

He took a deep breath and reached for her hand. "That must have been very hard on you," he said, giving her fingers a gentle squeeze. "Having your father leave you with a bunch of strangers like that."

"It . . . really wasn't as bad as you make it sound," she said.

Her voice had lost its bitter edge. It was back to being the voice of his erotic fantasies, smoke-tinged with a softly beguiling Southern drawl.

He felt his body begin to tighten again. His abdominal muscles started to constrict.

"In fact, it was kind of fun," she went on. "The other players had ice-cream cones sent in for us, then they took turns making us laugh with impressions of everyone from Ed Sullivan to Richard Nixon. Besides, what my father did that day isn't really the point here. He was addicted to cards, addicted to the need to play that one perfect game, and that addiction ended up killing him."

He was silent for a moment. "So why did you

take the job at the *Vicksburg Lady*, feeling the way you do about gambling?"

She held his gaze. "I had no choice."

He slowly ran his thumb across her knuckles, marveling at the softness of her skin, marveling, too, at how unbelievably pleasurable such a simple, innocuous act could be when shared with the right person.

"But we always have choices, Janie," he told her huskily. "Thinking we don't is just a cop-out."

She started to flush. "Yeah, well, not this time," she said, slipping her hand out of his grasp.

She leaned back in her chair and crossed her arms against her chest again. "You see, I'm a private investigator. Someone hired me to come to the *Vicksburg Lady*, otherwise I'd have never stepped foot on her gangplank."

He went immediately still. Whatever it was that he'd been expecting her to say, it certainly wasn't this.

"Are you telling me that someone hired you to investigate the *Lady?*" he asked.

"No. I'm telling you that someone hired me to locate a runaway heiress. She's seventeen but acts more like forty. After her father disapproved of the way she was dancing with her oversexed twenty-one-year-old boyfriend at a family shindig down at the country club, she split. The *Lady* was the last place she was spotted."

"So you think she will turn back up here?"

"Exactly. Probably sometime next weekend

since Seth—he's her boyfriend—likes to party it up on Saturday nights with a crap game. At any rate, I only took the job as a cocktail waitress as part of my cover. Discovering that some of the games were rigged was an accident, but I had no choice but to get involved once I did."

Not good, he decided. Not good at all. Having Jane Steele, private investigator, *get involved* with the problems on board the *Lady* was probably the last thing he needed, particularly since she seemed to have an ax to grind where casinos were concerned.

He supposed he could have identified himself as a Benedict right there on the spot, then asked her to back off and let him handle it from here on out, but he told himself that he still wasn't ready to level with her . . . or maybe it was just that he wasn't quite ready to have her look at him with the disgust that he knew his admission would likely generate from her. The only option he decided he had left was trying to keep close tabs on her investigation—and even closer tabs on his own libido because his hormones hadn't seemed to get the message that his brain was sending out loud and clear. Janie was just one *belleza* too dangerous to pursue.

"So how many of the games do you think are rigged?" he asked, forcing the thoughts back on track.

"One or two. Maybe more. And before you ask, yeah, I think Tidwell knows what's going on. In fact, I think he's masterminding the whole thing. I've been told that he instituted a lot of changes when he took over the management of the casino about six weeks ago. First up was a restructuring of the security procedure. He even had his girlfriend appointed acting chief of security when she didn't really have the qualifications for the job."

"Interesting," he murmured, wondering why no one at Benedict Casinos had been aware of this happening before now.

"Very," she agreed. "So, do you have any more questions, or can I ask a few of my own?"

He arched an eyebrow at her. "Oh, by all means, ask away."

She leaned forward slightly and placed her hands on the table. "Let's start with the basics, like who *you* are and what *you're* up to. And please don't tell me you're some high roller financier from the West Coast out here on holiday."

He grinned. "I see you've been one busy lady. You must have been quizzing the staff about me after you left Tidwell's office."

"Yeah," she said, giving him a frown. "Among other things . . . only I'm not nearly as gullible as Tidwell seems to be."

Then she nailed him with one of those coolly analytical gazes of hers.

"And you didn't answer my question," she reminded him. "Just who the devil are you, Nick Valdez?"

That toothpaste perfect smile of his only seemed to grow warmer, radiating a sensual heat that made even the marrow in her bones begin to boil like molten lava.

"Who am I?" he repeated, sounding amused.

"Exactly," she said, trying to ignore both his dimples and his laughing dark eyes—and the way they made her pulse race out of control.

It was no use, though. She couldn't ignore him, just as she couldn't ignore her own intense physical and undeniably emotional response to him. She couldn't ignore how he seemed to set fire to her blood with a single smile and make her sense of equilibrium desert her whenever he came close enough for her to catch a whiff of his cologne.

Nor could she seem to forget that all-too-brief kiss he'd given her a little over an hour earlier. She could still feel his lips brushing hers, still feel the hunger, the absolute need that he'd released inside her with a sweet rush of emotion, still feel her knees going as rubbery and useless as an old tire from a junk heap and her soul feeling somehow empty when he pulled away.

But the worst part wasn't the torrent of sexual desire that he could inspire inside her with a kiss. The worst part was the effect he seemed to have on her emotions. She couldn't believe that she'd told him so much about herself. She couldn't believe that she'd laid herself absolutely bare before him, sharing secrets and feelings about her father that she'd kept hidden for years, telling him things that she'd never even discussed with her sister, Kat.

Jane wanted to reassure herself that it wasn't Nick somehow, that it was the assignment, her having to come on board the *Vicksburg Lady* and being exposed to all the manufactured excitement of a casino again, that had triggered the emotional outburst. But she knew in her heart that it simply wasn't true.

It was Nick Valdez.

"But *cara*, you know who I am," he murmured, reaching for her hand again.

His fingers lightly stroked the curve of her wrist, sending white-hot tremors rocketing down her spine that left her trembling inside. Her throat felt parched, her knees suddenly wobbly.

Sweet heaven, she thought again. He was unraveling her very essence, one tiny sliver at a time, as if it were a piece of yarn . . . and she was just sitting there letting him do it.

She took a deep breath, then disengaged her hand from his again and rose to her feet. She started walking around the room, hoping the activity would help clear her head, get her back on track.

"I know who you say you are," she said, knowing her voice must sound husky, streaked with emotion. "But I'm having a little trouble believing you. You see, I've met my share of high rollers over the years. They're mostly weekend players. They know the game well enough to win a few hands, but they don't know it well enough to make their living at it."

"And you think I'm good enough to do that?"

He gave her that twin-dimpled smile of his again. She felt her heart begin to flutter.

"I'm flattered, Janie . . . especially since you've never even seen me play."

"I don't have to," she told him. "Your reaction to Will Pearce's poker game told me everything I needed to know about your skills."

He arched his eyebrows again and leaned back in his chair. "How so?"

"First, you noticed the deck was marked. Pearce didn't, nor did any of the other players at his table. Then you say you saw me switch Pearce's cards . . . I think it's more likely that you deduced I'd switched them because I'm too good ever to be seen."

He laughed. The sound was low and husky, reminding her of those sultry jazz sax solos again. She felt herself begin to flush.

She came to a stop next to the table. "And then there's the way you reacted to losing some money on a rigged roulette wheel. Rather than file a complaint with the gaming commission and leave the casino pronto, the way a typical weekend player would do, you decided to settle things by turning the tables on Tidwell in a private poker game. All of those added together mean you must be one of either two things."

His smile seemed to freeze in place. "And those two things are?"

"A professional card player whose ego can't stand being swindled," she said slowly. "Or someone from Benedict Casinos who wants to see how far Tidwell is willing to go before shutting him down."

His gaze didn't waver. "The addict or the pusher . . . not much of a choice, is it, considering how you feel about both?"

She shrugged.

"I admit I don't like being cheated," he went on. "Who does? But I'm not addicted to cards, *cara*. I've enjoyed the game from time to time, I even consider myself a damned good player, but gambling doesn't consume me . . . not the way it consumed your father."

He stood and took a step toward her. "And as for the other . . . well, you're the one planning to have the casino shut down, not me."

"The casino is running crooked games. It deserves to be shut down."

"Tidwell deserves to be shut down," he corrected. "Big difference. By your own admission, only a handful of games on board the *Lady* are suspect. Having her shut down amounts to overkill."

"Excuse me?"

Now it was his turn to shrug. "It's like putting a thoroughbred down when he bruises his leg, rather than bandaging him up and letting him get some rest. What about the big picture? What about the hundreds of employees who'll be thrown out of work if the *Lady* closes, or the loss of revenue to the community?"

She scowled. "What about the hundreds of people who've probably already been ripped off by the casino? What about the hundreds more who are next in line to be scammed? What about *that* big picture?"

"Tidwell's the one you should be going after," he said quietly. "Not the *Vicksburg Lady*. Hell, I agree that he should be stopped. In fact, I'm willing to set aside my own plans and do whatever it takes to help you nail the slimy bastard."

"Thanks, but I don't need any help."

He gave her a soft smile. "Oh, but I think you do. I think you need all the help that you can come by. You've been here what? Twenty-four hours? So far, you've risked your neck cheating at cards for a stranger, probably had your heroics videotaped by the security camera, and then there's your two attempts at breaking and entering to retrieve the evidence of your good deed. Both have nearly met with complete and total disaster."

She blushed. Dammit, but he *would* have to remind her about that.

"Besides, if you don't agree to join forces with me," he went on, flashing those dimples at her again, "I'll have to seek justice my way. I'll probably try to win back my money in the card game . . . probably get caught too. Who knows what Tidwell may force me into telling him? I may even accidentally blow your cover before they dump my poor battered body somewhere down the river. Now, do you really want that on your conscience, *cara*?"

She scowled at him. "Fine. You've made your point. Quite succinctly, in fact."

"So you agree that we should work together?"

A few seconds passed.

Jane sighed. She told herself that she'd probably end up regretting what she was about to do. Even so, she really didn't see where she had much choice in the matter, despite Nick's lecture to the contrary that one always had options. He'd been wrong, anyway. There were times when you were simply stuck between that rock and the hard place and there was nothing much to be done about it other than accept it.

And this, unfortunately, appeared to be one of those times.

"Yeah," she said. "I agree."

Forty-five minutes later, after having a quick dinner of hamburgers and french fries ordered from room service, Jane sat on the edge of Nick's bed, trying her damnedest not to watch the play of corded muscles that rippled along the curve of his back as he finished hooking up the portable VCR to the television set.

Simply telling herself not to watch him was a lot easier than actually being able not to do so. Besides, he had removed his jacket. Thanks to his form-hugging black collarless silk shirt and black wool trousers, she had a clear, unobstructed view of his flat-as-a-washboard stomach and broad masculine shoulders.

She watched as he knelt down on the floor to plug the machine into the wall socket.

He also had a nicely rounded derriere.

Jane felt herself flush again.

This was getting ridiculous, she thought. She was gawking at the man like some lovestruck teen-age girl when she ought to be concentrating on the case that she'd just taken on pro bono.

She took a slow, deep breath, then reached for her diet soda on the nightstand. "It, ah, was nice of Tidwell to loan you the machine." She took a long sip.

Nick glanced over his shoulder and gave her a grin. "Yeah, well, lucky for us he likes to keep his prospective pigeons happy."

They'd decided to watch the tape before mapping out their strategy for busting Tidwell's con game. Nick had pointed out, and she'd agreed, that she'd need evidence of the rigged games before presenting her case to the gaming commission; if the poker game had been taped, along with her intervention, the purloined cassette would go a long way toward providing that evidence. But to watch the tape, they'd needed a videocassette player.

No problem, Nick had said, then he'd telephoned the front desk to request they provide him with a VCR. The machine had been delivered less than ten minutes later by the assistant desk clerk who'd treated Nick as if he were visiting royalty.

"Okay," Nick said. "Let's see what we've really got here."

He slipped the videocassette into the machine, then turned and walked around the king-size bed to take his seat across from her.

"Do you have the remote?" he asked.

"I . . ." She glanced from side to side. She didn't see it.

"Never mind, I found it."

He leaned toward her and made a grab for the slim black box which was lodged under the pillow next to her. His shoulder lightly brushed against hers in passing and she froze, trying not to move a muscle, trying to ignore the heat of his body as it rushed over her, threatening to scorch her soul with its intensity, trying to ignore the masculine scent of his cologne as it swamped her senses and left her feeling dizzy and slightly off balance, trying to ignore him.

She'd have probably had more success trying to ignore the law of gravity.

Nick settled back against his pillows. "About how far back do you think I should rewind?" he asked, sounding so damned normal that she wanted to slug him.

Instead, she finished off her soda, toying with the idea of asking him to turn on the air-conditioning even though it was the dead of winter outside.

"Try, ah, about fifteen minutes' worth," she

said, wondering if her voice sounded as breathless as she suddenly felt.

"All the tapes were changed shortly after I left the poker table," she added.

He nodded and pressed the rewind button. The machine began to whir for a long moment, then Nick pressed a series of buttons and the machine made a soft clicking sound as the tape moved into the play mode. Then, static—loud, unrelenting static—filled the screen.

"Are you sure that you hooked everything up correctly?" she asked.

He frowned. "Pretty sure. I have a unit similar to it at home."

He slid off the bed and walked over to the VCR. He pressed a couple of buttons on the VCR's front panel and the tape popped out. Then he checked the cables on the back of the machine, rechecked the hookup to the television, and slid the tape back into the VCR to try again.

Still no picture. Only the same annoying static from before.

Puzzled, Jane slid off the bed and walked over to join him, careful, though, to keep herself far enough away from him to protect her equilibrium.

"What do you think?" she asked. "Is it a defective tape?"

He shrugged. "Maybe, although if I didn't know better, I'd say that this one had either been erased or was never recorded on at all. I'm placing my money on the latter."

The same possibility had occurred to her, although it didn't make much sense. Why would the surveillance unit go to all the trouble of creating the illusion that they were recording their video feed when it would have been far simpler to omit the areas where the rigged games were being played?

He turned off the machine. "Now what?"

"Back to square one, I guess."

"The surveillance room?"

She nodded. "The surveillance room."

A third attempt at breaking and entering into the casino might be pressing her already shaky luck past its limit—even without the addition of a new *partner* who seemed to make her brain short-circuit whenever he stood too close to her.

Jane glanced at Nick who was already shrugging into his jacket . . . looking so damned good doing it, too, that it nearly stole her breath away.

She frowned and reached for her coat.

Ten to one, they'd never even make it past the service stairwell without getting busted.

FOUR

"Well, at least now I know how you're able to slip past all those locked doors."

Grinning, Nick leaned against the wall next to Jane and watched her expertly manipulate two thin metal picks into the lock of the surveillance room with a skill that would have done a professional thief proud.

"I was beginning to think that you weren't a flesh-and-blood woman," he said. "The way you'd suddenly pop up in a wet bar when I started thinking about you . . . I figured you must be part *bruja.*"

"Bruja?"

She repeated the word in that soft Southern drawl of hers, making it sound far sexier than he'd have ever imagined possible.

"What's that supposed to be?" she asked. "Or do I not want to know?"

He smiled. "It's a sorceress . . . a witch . . . someone skilled in the mysterious and magical ways of the necromancer."

He still wasn't all that sure she wasn't some *bruja*, either . . . or at least a dark-haired enchantress sent to test his self-control the way those knights of the Round Table were often tested in all the Arthurian legends he'd had to read about in junior high school. Hell, in the few hours that he'd known her, Jane Steele had woven a spell around him that not even all of Merlin's magic potions could have broken.

She blushed, which only seemed to make his heart beat faster somehow.

"Knowing how to pick a lock is hardly a feat of magic, Nick," she said.

The door popped open, and she gave him a triumphant smile.

"In fact, once you know how to do it," she went on, "it's really quite easy."

She inserted the lock picks back into their carrying case and ducked inside the small lounge with Nick fast behind her.

Embarrassingly easy would have been more accurate, he decided.

He closed the door and followed her into the surveillance room, where she'd already begun to check out the recording equipment. Being able to break in to one of the casino's nerve centers should have been next to impossible, yet this was the second time that Jane had done it that night alone.

Corporate policy was quite clear on the subject of the casino's three surveillance rooms too. They were to be staffed twenty-four hours a day, no exceptions, but according to Jane's source, Tidwell had cut the number of personnel assigned to the unit in half upon his promotion, stating that it was a waste of both money and man power. Then he'd done the unthinkable by encouraging the guards to take their breaks at the same time.

More likely than not, Tidwell didn't want to run the risk of having security spot any of the rigged games he had going up on deck. But that was beside the point, Nick thought. Tidwell had been able to reduce the security personnel and rig the games because someone at corporate had gotten lazy and not followed up on what was happening at the casino.

For that matter, Benedict Casinos might have still been unaware of the damage Tidwell was wreaking in Mississippi, both to the casino's reputation and to its revenues, if Nick's father hadn't received a letter from an irate lady from Centreville, a small town in the southwestern portion of the state. The woman had been convinced she'd been ripped off to the tune of twenty dollars in one of the *Lady*'s slot machines.

Even though Sid suspected the woman may have been a sore loser, he'd refunded her money—twenty dollars was a small price to pay for goodwill—and asked Nick to look things over at the casino on his trip to Mississippi.

Nick figured that when he told his father what he'd uncovered—about the rigged games and the sloppy security procedures on board the *Lady*—those nuclear test explosions in Nevada back in the forties would seem a relatively mild outburst by comparison.

"You've gotten awfully quiet all of a sudden," Jane murmured, eyeing him speculatively from the row of recording equipment. "Having second thoughts about our partnership already?"

"Not a chance, *cara*."

He gave her another grin.

"In fact, I was just standing here thinking about you," he added.

It wasn't a lie outright, he reassured himself, crossing over to where she stood. It was more like an exaggeration of the truth. Because Jane had been occupying his thoughts since the moment he'd first seen her.

"Tell me something," he went on. "Is using a lock pick another one of those little parlor tricks that your father taught you?"

"Uh-uh."

She glanced back at the video recorder.

"I have a friend who's a retired jewel thief . . . Mike's been giving me lessons."

"You've been getting lessons on using a lock pick from a jewel thief?"

Once again, she'd said something that he hadn't been expecting her to say.

"*Retired* jewel thief," she corrected him. "Mike's

completely legit now . . . owns a company called Emerald Security down in New Orleans. They're one of the best in the business too."

"I see," he murmured, although he did nothing of the kind. No matter how he tried, he couldn't quite picture his Janie spending her off-duty hours hanging around known felons.

He started to frown. "And this . . . Mike, did you call him? . . . He's what to you, exactly? Just a good pal or a boyfriend . . . what?"

Her lips curled in a smile but she didn't look up.

"Idle curiosity, Mr. Valdez?" she asked. "Or something of a more personal interest?"

"Maybe a little of both."

Even as he said it, Nick told himself that he was out of line. She was off-limits, for more reasons than he could count, yet he couldn't seem to help himself from wanting to know more about her.

He couldn't deny the wave of unadulterated jealousy that had washed over him when he heard her talk about this former jewel thief-cum-hotshot security specialist of hers.

"I admit that I'm worried about you," he told her quietly. "Jewel thieves . . . even retired ones . . . are used to living a certain kind of life-style that tends to make them . . . well, a poor relationship choice for a woman like you."

She leveled those cool sea-green eyes of hers at him again. "And what kind of woman do you think I am? Particularly dim-witted or just terribly naive?"

"No," he said quickly. "I . . . trust me, Janie. I

think your wits are about as sharp as they get, and you've never struck me as being naive. I just meant that you're smart and brave and loyal."

Most of all, she was the kind of woman a man could find himself getting serious about . . . if he was so inclined to be looking for that sort of thing, which Nick assured himself he was not.

"Smart?" Jane mumbled. "Brave and loyal? Jeez, you make me sound like Lassie."

He laughed. "Then I guess I'm not explaining myself very well," he said. "It's just that you . . . well, you jeopardized your own safety to help a stranger tonight, and you did it without ever telling him that you were his guardian angel. That kind of thing doesn't happen very often, at least not in casinos. I think you're special, *cara*."

She frowned. "Yeah, and I think you're full of it, Nick Valdez."

He frowned back.

"I mean, how could you possibly have had time to form an opinion as to whether or not I'm ordinary or unique?" she went on. "You just met me a couple of hours ago."

Then she dropped her gaze back to the recorder where she started to work on one of its components.

"You've got a point, I suppose," he said. "But sometimes it's not the amount of time that you know a person that counts, it's the quality of the time you spend with them . . . after all, you formed an opinion about me just as quickly, didn't you?" And it was an opinion that he wished he could convince her to change, even though he felt it was partially justified.

His jab seemed to get her attention. She raised her head and stared at him for a moment.

"Okay," she said, lowering the lock pick she was using as a makeshift screwdriver. "I'll bite. Just whom do you think would make a better . . . what was it that you called it again?"

"Relationship choice," he told her.

"Right. Just whom do you think would be a better relationship choice for me? Some kind of a professional gambler, perhaps?"

"Either someone like that or a casino executive." He held her gaze. "Yeah, I could see that happening. Very easily, in fact."

He could see it so easily, because he'd been fantasizing about it happening ever since he'd met her.

She scowled. "Then you should get your vision checked. Pronto."

"Maybe," he said. "I mean, I know how you feel about people in the business but . . . hypothetically speaking . . . what if I told you that there was this man . . . a real nice guy some would say . . . who'd once lived that kind of life but had walked away? That he wanted a new life now, somewhere far from all the poker tables and roulette wheels. Would it change your position any?"

"Not a whole lot, no," she said coldly. "You see, my father used to give me the same speech at least once a month. It's kind of lost its charm for me."

A few seconds passed.

"Then I guess those kind of people wouldn't be right for you, would they?" he asked.

She didn't answer him.

He regarded her for a moment longer, then sighed.

"*Cara*, I'm sorry," he said. "It's just that I like you . . . I wouldn't want to see you get hurt."

She blushed again. "Well, you can stop worrying about me. I don't have a boyfriend, nor am I in the market for one. Steele Angel Investigations is about all the commitment I can handle at the moment. And as for my friend, Mike . . ."

She replaced the backing of the recorder and tightened its screws with the blunt side of her lock pick.

"Mike is short for Michael Ann," she explained. "She got married ten months ago to her former partner, and she might very well argue with you over whether or not reformed thieves make good relationship material. She and Remy are expecting twins this June."

Nick started to relax and gave her a smile. "Michael Ann, huh? I guess this is where I try and remove my rather large foot from my mouth and apologize to you. Again."

"You can save them both for later," she said, returning the lock pick to its case which she then dropped into her uniform pocket.

She pointed to the recorder she'd been working on. "I think I found the problem with our tape," she went on, refocusing his attention back to the reason they were there. The mystery of the blank security tape.

"Someone's modified the machine so that it doesn't record," she said. "All the others on the row seem fine, though."

"So you think all the rigged games are covered by the same monitor?"

He glanced at the wall of monitors. The video image being displayed on the screen in question just then was of a bank of slot machines.

"That's my guess," she said. "Of course, we won't know for sure until we check out the five security cameras hooked up to the monitor."

He nodded. "Then let's do it."

"Fine," Jane murmured, then glanced back at the monitors. "We can start with the slot machines. I think these are . . . *sonofabitch!*"

Nick followed her gaze to the wall of monitors, scanning the images until he found the one that she was staring at in horror . . . the video screen whose feed came from the security camera in the hallway just outside.

The two surveillance room guards Nick had spoken with earlier—who were now supposed to be somewhere safely up on deck having their dinner, at least for another good fifteen minutes or so—had just turned the corner and were making their way down the long hall, presumably on their way back to their post.

Nick muttered a particularly colorful expletive of his own and grabbed her hand.

"Come on," he said, hurrying her back into the adjacent lounge.

"Where to? There's no place to go."

Nick closed the door to the surveillance room and considered their options. Jane was right. There weren't any other exits. The only way in—and out—was the door leading into the same hallway that the guards were currently walking down, and there were no convenient wet bars lying about for them to hide in, either.

That meant they'd have to stand their ground. To do so, they needed to come up with an explanation—a brilliant one—for their presence in an area of the riverboat considered strictly off-limits.

The faster they came up with it the better, since the guards would likely be there any second.

Nick yanked off his coat and jacket and tossed both onto the scarred oak coffee table. Then he peeled off his loafers.

"Take off your coat," he said, unbuttoning his silk shirt. "Your shoes too."

She scowled at him. "Whatever for?"

"I've got an idea." He took her arm and led her over to the brown plaid sofa. "We don't have a lot of time to argue about this."

"Okay, okay."

She shrugged off her coat, which she tossed next to his, and kicked off her shoes. The black high heels landed on different sections of the carpeted floor.

"Just please don't tell me that you're planning to try and fake them out by saying we slipped in here for a quick kiss," she muttered. "That's all I ask."

He undid his belt, unzipped his pants, and fell back on the sofa, taking her with him. She landed on top of him with a gasp of surprise and a splash of her long silky hair against his face.

"I wouldn't dream of it," he told her huskily. "We both know that a mere kiss wouldn't be nearly enough to convince anybody."

The scent of lilacs and springtime and something damn near close to heaven swirled around him, making his breath catch in his throat. *¡Válgame Dios!* He hadn't been prepared for how good it would feel to hold her against him . . . to feel her breasts, so firm and yet so soft, pressing invitingly against his chest.

Her talented little hands, hands that could pick locks and switch cards in a crooked poker game with ease, hands that were now resting on his shoulders, seared their palm prints through the thin fabric of his shirt to brand his soul with her touch. Her slender hips and thighs fitted against him so beautifully, and her very closeness sent a liquefied heat racing through his veins, arousing him to the point of insanity itself.

Maybe . . . he . . . should rethink their strategy here, he decided, feeling his body begin to tighten until his erection strained against his under-shorts.

After all, this was only supposed to be a bit of make-believe for the benefit of the guards. This wasn't real . . . even if his body was having trouble telling the difference.

"This . . . isn't going to work," she said in a smoke-tinged whisper that echoed his own sentiments even as it spun his imagination further out of control. "I mean, how stupid do you think these guys are?"

He grasped her waist and pulled her toward him until she straddled his hips. A stab of awareness, of hunger, shot straight through him as he felt their bodies make contact beneath their clothes. Feeling as though he were about to come undone right there on the spot, he squeezed his eyes closed for a moment and tried to suppress a shudder, which he couldn't. Then he shifted her slightly until she was resting atop his hip.

"For our sakes, *cara,*" he whispered, "I hope they're very stupid."

Then, deciding he'd gone too far into their charade to stop now even if he'd wanted to, Nick started to moan as loudly as he could while rocking her hips suggestively against him, trying his damnedest to create the illusion that they were caught in the throes of a wild, all-consuming passion.

Only for him, Nick thought, pulling her closer, it wasn't all that far removed from the truth.

Jane decided that Nick had lost his mind.

She also decided that she'd lost hers as well since she was matching him theatrical moan for theatrical moan, simulated thrust for simulated thrust, even though she knew their crazy stunt was never going to work, not in a million years. No one was stupid enough to believe that she and Nick had been so overcome by raw desire that they'd ducked into the employee lounge adjacent a top security area to have a quickie because that kind of thing never happened in real life.

That's when he skimmed his fingers over her back, searing through the nylon fabric of her uniform as though his fingertips were an open flame, sending dozens of fire-laced streaks shooting through her. His touch energized her soul and left her close to trembling. Then his mouth settled over hers again, lips brushing lips in the sweetest kiss imaginable, a kiss that seemed certain to send her recently made resolution to keep him at a safe emotional distance spiraling down in an explosion of white-hot flames if she wasn't careful to guard against it.

But how could she guard herself against such unrelenting pleasure? How could she resist the sweet temptation of his touch?

Once again, she was reminded of the conflicting images that kissing Nick brought to mind . . . of angel and of demon . . . of gentleness and of un-

bearable heat . . . of a satisfaction deep inside her
and of an insatiable, endless hunger.

It was too much.

She softly moaned, not faking it this time, and
surrendered to the feeling for a moment, sliding her
hands up his chest to touch his face.

His skin felt warm and bristled with a slight
beard. She stroked his cheeks, luxuriating in the
rustle of those baby whiskers beneath her fingers,
until the kiss slowed and began to deepen . . . until she felt the warm pressure of his tongue against
her lips and she opened for him.

Her heart started to pound as their tongues
made contact. It was . . . perfect. Then he rubbed
his tongue against hers, caressing, massaging, enticing until their tongues started to move together in a
dizzyingly erotic dance that left her breathless and
consumed by a fever unlike any she'd ever felt before.

She realized then that she'd been wrong, so
wrong that she even felt foolish about it. It *was*
possible to become enslaved enough to one's libido,
to one's desire, that a few moments of physical pleasure would be worth any risk.

She shuddered against him.

Dear God, she thought. What was happening to
her? She wanted this man, needed him with a passion so intense, it could overwhelm both her inhibitions and thirty years' worth of carefully controlled
emotions.

Then a key started to rattle in the lock.

Nick broke the kiss and slid his hands over her hips, pulling her closer.

"It's show time, *cara*," he murmured.

His voice was little more than a husky whisper.

"I . . . I still think this is a bad idea," she whispered back, although her reasons for feeling that way had certainly changed.

The door began to open.

"Too late," he whispered again.

Then he started to intensify the fervor of his simulated thrusts, shifting their performance into high gear.

"That's it, baby," he cooed. "Just . . . like that. Oh, yeah."

He said the words in a loud, throaty moan that seemed torn from his soul.

Jane forced herself to swing back into character as well, echoing his cries of imitation passion.

Then she felt the curve of Nick's hip rubbing against her through her cotton panties. They were rapid, directed strokes that sent a shock wave of pure pleasure crashing around her.

"I . . . oh my God!" she gasped. She shuddered against him again.

This was madness, she decided. Or just a case of supreme idiocy. Either way, it was far worse than all the other incredibly stupid mistakes she'd made that evening combined. While Nick's faked moans only grew louder, and his pretend lovemaking more aggressive, she felt as if she were simply burning alive.

Time seemed suspended for a moment, then she

heard Fitzpatrick—or perhaps it was his partner—mutter something unintelligible under his
breath.

At any rate, Nick's response was immediate.

He swore bitterly in Spanish, then he tried to
scramble into a sitting position, only to give the
back of the sofa a deliberate shove with his knee
that propelled them both off the edge of the couch
toward the floor.

Jane cried out and made a grab for his shoulders,
but his grasp on her hips held her tight.

They dropped to the carpet as a single unit, with
him on the bottom and her on top. Only she was
completely on top of him this time, her knees straddling his hips, her groin joined to his. Their bodies
were so carefully aligned, she could feel his erection
resting against her—and the shudder that shook
him at the discovery of where she'd landed after
their mad tumble off the sofa.

Their gazes locked for a moment.

Nick drew a sharp intake of breath and slowly
eased her off him, taking extraordinary care to keep
the hem of her uniform pulled down over her
thighs. Again, he tried to sit up, pretended he
couldn't do it, then slumped back against the sofa.

"¡*Válgame Dios!* Don't you people believe in
knocking before entering a room?"

His voice was rough around the edges, streaked
with emotion.

Jane raked her hair back and waited for her
heart rate to return to normal. She glanced at the

guards, trying to gauge their reaction to what they'd found, expecting skepticism if not outright disbelief.

Instead, they were grinning, looking more amused than anything else.

"Why the hell should we knock?" Fitzpatrick's partner asked. "You're trespassin' in a high security area. We could have both your butts thrown into jail on half a dozen charges if we want to."

"High security area?"

Nick fumbled with the zipper of his pants and winced as though he were in pain.

"I, ah, thought this was just an employee break room of some kind," he said. "We didn't see any off-limit signs posted anywhere around here."

"Yeah, well, Mr. Valdez," Fitzpatrick said. "This entire section of the riverboat is off-limits."

Mr. Valdez?

Jane shot a surprised glance at Nick. How did the guard know Nick's name? she wondered.

Realizing that she probably wouldn't like the answer, she returned her attention to Fitzpatrick just as he was glancing at her.

"Your, ah, *date* here should have known better," Fitzpatrick added dryly.

She shook her head. "But I didn't know. No one told me that we weren't supposed to be down here. I . . . today's my first day. I'm sorry."

She decided that her lie sounded convincing, mostly because her voice sounded strangely husky to her own ears, almost unrecognizable.

Fitzpatrick's partner laughed. "This is your first day? Well, I hate to be the one to break it to you, sugar, but this is probably going to be your *last* day working at the *Lady* too."

"'Now wait a minute," Nick said, sitting up. "This wasn't Jane's fault. It was mine. I'll take full responsibility for any repercussions that our . . . little *indiscretion* . . . may cause."

The guard shrugged, then twisted the doorknob and eyed them again, more suspiciously this time.

"How'd you two get in here, anyway?" he asked.

"How did we . . . ?"

Nick took a deep breath and started again. "How the hell do you think we got in here? We opened the door and walked in."

"You mean the door was unlocked?"

The question came from Fitzpatrick. He turned to his partner. "Dammit, Landon, you left the friggin' door unlocked! If Weems hears about *that*, our own bacon is gonna be fried."

Landon scowled back. "What do you mean *I* left the door unlocked? You were there, too, man. Remember?"

Then the two men got into a sharply worded argument over whose fault it was the door had been left unlocked, ignoring both her and Nick for a moment.

"'Hey . . . *amigos*!" Nick ran his hand through his short-cropped hair. "Are you through with us here? 'Cause if you are, the lady and I would like to leave."

He motioned toward her. "This is a little . . . well, embarrassing, you know?" he went on, dropping his voice lower.

The two guards stopped in middebate.

"Ah, sure, Mr. Valdez," Fitzpatrick said, looking a little flustered himself. "No problem. Just stay out of this section of the *Vicksburg Lady* in the future, okay?"

"Yeah, and try to conduct all of your, ah . . . *business* . . . back at your room," added Landon with a wide grin. "That way, it'll be less embarrassing for everybody concerned."

Then the guards crossed over to the surveillance room and slipped inside without another word. They closed the door quietly behind them.

Seconds later, the echo of their continued argument over whose responsibility it was to lock the hallway door filtered back into the lounge.

Jane collapsed against the bottom of the sofa with a long sigh. "I . . . don't . . . believe it," she murmured under her breath.

Nick gave her a grin. "Yeah, well, believe it, *cara*," he told her in a low whisper. "We pulled it off, just like I told you we would."

Then he reached past her to grab his coat and jacket from the coffee table, giving her shoulder a casual brush that sent a shiver of longing and need straight through to her core.

"Maybe next time you'll trust me when I tell you that I've got a plan," he said.

Next time?

She felt herself flush straight down to her toes. Once with Nick Valdez was bad enough, she decided.

A second time would probably kill her.

She scrambled to her feet. "Yeah, well, don't bet on it," she whispered back, retrieving her shoes. "I don't think I'll have much need for any more of your *plans*, thank you very much."

Shock registered across his much too handsome face. "I . . . don't think I follow you."

"I mean, there's not going to be any next time for us," she said, spelling it out for him as carefully as she could. "Our partnership has just been dissolved."

She grabbed her coat and shoes and rushed out into the hallway before he could reply.

She rushed out before she could lose whatever tenuous grip she still may have had on her sanity and change her mind, both about their partnership and her vow of never becoming emotionally involved with a professional gambler. Because, heaven help her, she was coming close to doing both.

Dangerously close, in fact.

FIVE

When Jane reported to work at eleven the following morning, she realized that she and Nick had perhaps been a tad premature in thinking they'd gotten away with their break-in of the surveillance room. A message from Robert Tidwell was waiting for her at the time clock.

Actually, it was more like an imperial summons commanding her to appear before him in his office immediately upon her arrival at the casino.

"Damn," she whispered to herself. She crumpled the note and shoved it into the pocket of her coat.

She considered cutting her losses and hightailing it out of the casino while she still could, but decided against it. She had too much invested, in both the Traynor case and her own pro bono investigation of the *Vicksburg Lady*, to fold now. Besides, if Tidwell had caught on to what she was up to and was planning to take her on some nonreturnable cruise down the Mississippi, he'd have sent a couple of guards to retrieve her, rather than leave a note for her at the time clock.

Five minutes later, Jane stood outside Tidwell's office, straightening the looped belt of her coat and trying to buoy her flagging self-confidence. Afraid she might lose her nerve if she put it off any longer, she rapped her knuckles against the door.

"Come in."

She took a deep breath to slow the rapid pounding of her heart—she now knew how Daniel felt when he was about to enter the lion's den—and opened the door. Tidwell was seated behind his desk, smoking another cigar.

He looked up and gave her a smile that was all teeth and gums. It was a smile so unquestionably leonine, so in sync with her thoughts, that it made her want to jump right out of her skin.

"Thank you for coming down here so promptly, Jane," he said. "May I call you Jane?"

"Ah, sure." She closed the door behind her.

He smiled again. "Please, have a seat. Would you like some coffee?"

A silver-plated coffeepot sat on his desk, along with two china cups in their saucers. She nodded and slowly sat down while he poured them both a cup. The scent of chicory wafted over to her.

"I'm sure you know why I wanted to talk to you this morning," he said quietly.

"I've . . . got . . . a pretty good idea," she

said, peeling off her gloves, which she then tucked into the pocket of her coat.

"I understand there was an incident last night," he went on. "A romantic tryst below deck between you and one of the casino's patrons, a gentleman from Las Vegas named Nick Valdez. Is this correct?"

Jane slowly stirred artificial sweetener into her coffee and weighed her options, wondering when—or if—Tidwell was going to confront her about the poker game, the missing videotape, and the location of her so-called *romantic tryst* with Nick. She also wondered why Barbara Weems wasn't in the room with Tidwell . . . and if this was a positive sign or an indication that now would be a good time to start worrying in earnest.

Deciding that she had nothing to lose, Jane gave her and Nick's momentarily-swept-away-by-passion cover one last shot.

"I'm sorry, Mr. Tidwell," she said. "I know company policy is quite explicit about these kinds of things, and I . . . I really don't have any excuse for my behavior. It's just—"

"Relax," Tidwell said, interrupting her. "You don't need to explain what happened. You're an attractive young woman . . . he's an attractive young man. Sometimes the call of nature can get the better of our common sense. I'm sure you didn't mean to jeopardize the security of the casino by sneaking a professional gambler below deck."

"I . . . no, I didn't," she said.

He sipped his coffee and scrutinized her over the edge of the cup, like a lion contemplating a gazelle he was planning to have for lunch.

"And I'm also sure that you won't repeat the mistake of engaging in those . . . shall we say, amorous activities . . . here on the casino premises in the future?"

She felt herself flush. "Absolutely not," she said, dropping her gaze. "In fact, I've already told Nick . . . Mr. Valdez . . . that we're through."

She heard Tidwell cluck his tongue in disapproval.

"That's too bad, Jane," he said. "Is there no chance then of your changing your mind and going out with him again?"

The hairs began to prickle along the nape of her neck. She raised her head to meet his gaze.

"You have my word, Mr. Tidwell, that there won't be any repeat performances of last night."

"So you've said," Tidwell murmured dryly. "But what I'm asking you, honey, is something entirely different. Do you still find Nick Valdez attractive or don't you?"

Did she still find him attractive?

Memories flooded back, memories of Nick's face, of his laughing dark eyes, twin-dimpled smile, and much too kissable lips. Memories of those same lips slowly moving over hers . . . of his tongue gliding around hers, caressing, massaging, enticing her beyond all reason . . .

Memories, too, of his arousal, so firm and hard,

pressing against her for the briefest moment, yet long enough to communicate a desire whose power made her tremble still.

"I . . . I suppose so." she said huskily.

Oh, who was she trying to kid? she asked herself. She'd never been as attracted to a man in her entire life as she was to Nick Valdez. Telling herself that she was wrong to feel that way, that getting involved with an inveterate gambler would only end up breaking her heart, did little to change those feelings.

She was already involved with him, had been from the moment his lips had first brushed over hers.

Hell, if she didn't know better, she'd think she was beginning to fall in love with the man.

"Good," Tidwell said. "That's what I wanted to hear you say. You see, Mr. Valdez is a guest of the casino. A very *important* guest. I want to do everything in my power to make him happy."

He flicked ash into the tray on his desk and took a sip of coffee.

"And it appears that you make him happy, Jane . . . or at least you did last night before the guards caught you both."

She felt her cheeks start to flame. "So . . . what, exactly, are you asking me to do? Go out on a date with him?"

Tidwell laughed. "Oh, I want you to do more than that, Jane. Until further notice, your duties here at the casino—your *only* duties here at the casino—will be entertaining Mr. Valdez . . . in any way he chooses."

Jane stared at him in disbelief. She wasn't sure whether a judge would construe his suggestion to be simple sexual harassment or forced prostitution. Either way, Tidwell had just sunk to a new level of sleaze.

"And if I refuse my new . . . *assignment?*" she asked slowly. "What happens then?"

His smile faded. "Well, then I would have no choice but to terminate your employment here at the *Vicksburg Lady* and recommend that the local authorities prosecute you for criminal trespass. But I see no reason to resort to those unpleasantries . . . do you, Jane?"

She felt herself go completely cold. Still, she gave him her best smile.

"No reason at all," she murmured. "It'll be my pleasure to entertain Mr. Valdez."

It would be an even bigger pleasure to see both Tidwell and the *Vicksburg Lady* permanently shut down . . . which she fully intended to do, regardless of what it might take.

Jane stopped at the ladies' lounge to use the pay phone on her way back upstairs and placed a couple of telephone calls.

The first one was to her office to check in. After filling in her partner John on the status of the Traynor case—namely, that she would have to wait until the weekend before Seth and Marybeth made an appearance at the casino, if they made one at all—Jane told him briefly about what she'd discovered on board the *Lady* and of her decision to gather the evidence necessary to have the casino closed by the gaming commission.

Ignoring his question about who she thought would be funding her investigation—those years she'd spent haranguing him into playing things strictly by the book had apparently paid off—she asked him to have their resident computer whiz run a complete background check on Robert Tidwell.

Jane figured that the man couldn't have sprouted into full-grown human scum overnight; finding out where Tidwell had worked before the *Lady*, and if he had a record of running similar scams in other casinos, would go a long way toward building her case.

After receiving an assurance from Johnny that she'd have the information she requested within forty-eight hours—seventy-two at the outside—she placed her second call to Nick's room. He wasn't in, so she left a message and went to find him.

They had a lot to discuss.

First was the reinstatement of their partnership, which he might not even agree with after the way she'd bailed out on him the night before. Then, there was the most important topic of all—finding the best way to keelhaul Tidwell.

The sooner they got the job done, the better she'd like it too.

❖————————❖

Nick dropped three more coins into the dollar slot machine that he'd watched on the video monitor down in the surveillance room the night before, and pulled its large, ornately carved handle. The tumblers began to roll. He thought he detected a momentary hesitation in the machine before two cherries and a bar fell into place across the view panel.

Coins clanked into the metal bin, but not many. By his calculations, he was down a good hundred and fifty in his experiment that morning. The other machines on the row seemed fine, but not this one. It was far from it, in fact. Even allowing for an unusually long streak of bad luck, the payout ratio was entirely too low, which could only mean one thing. Jane's suspicions about the malfunctioning video recorder being linked to the rigged games on board the *Lady* were probably true.

He reached into the slot machine's basin and removed the five coins, then dropped them into his mostly empty red-and-black plastic bucket, feeling his thoughts begin to drift, as always, toward the enigmatic Ms. Steele.

The woman was going to drive him stark raving mad, he decided with a frown. One minute she was melting against him in the most emotionally satisfying kiss he'd ever experienced . . . slowly stroking her fingertips over his face until he shuddered, making him feel more wanted, more desired with a single touch than he could have thought humanly possible.

One minute, she was his own personal *bruja*, bewitching both his body and his heart with the sound of her smoke-tinged voice . . . seducing his very soul with a voice that conjured up images of the two of them, stripped of both their clothes and their inhibitions, making wildly passionate love for half an eternity or so.

And the next . . .

He drew a deep breath, then slowly exhaled.

Well, the next minute, she was spitting at him like a cat who'd just been dunked in a pail of water and was none too pleased by it.

Dammit, but he couldn't figure her out, nor could he figure out why she seemed to affect him the way she did. *¡Dios!* he thought, taking another deep breath. He'd already wasted half the night thinking about her. He had no intention of wasting the whole day as well.

But he couldn't seem to help himself from thinking about her. Not now . . . and certainly not the night before when he'd lain in bed for hours, replaying their performance in the employees' lounge, one slow frame at a time, trying to determine what he could have possibly done to make her turn on him the way she had.

Granted, he'd gotten a little aggressive in their pretend lovemaking session, but their act had to look authentic or the guards would've never bought it. He'd assumed that Jane had known that because she'd gone along with his plan. As for when their faked make-out session had ceased being a game for him . . .

He felt his body begin to tighten at the memory of Jane straddling his hips, of her full, rounded breasts pressing so intimately against his chest, of their tongues finally doing that slow, erotic tango he'd been fantasizing about for what seemed to have been almost forever.

He sighed. Yeah, he had enjoyed their little stage show all right, but he suspected that she'd enjoyed it just as much.

Now that he thought about it, he could have hit on the reason why Jane had severed their newly formed partnership without so much as a word of explanation and bolted for the door.

Nick dropped another three coins into the slot and pulled the handle. The tumblers rolled again, only this time three blanks fell into place across the view screen.

No payout at all.

It was sort of like the way his luck had been running with Jane.

"Sugar, you'd better stop feeding that machine all your money. It don't look like today's your lucky day, not that mine's been all that much better."

The advice came from the elderly woman sitting at the slot machine next to him.

He gave her a smile. "You're probably right. But my luck's never been much good on these things anyway." He leaned in closer. "You know, they don't call them one-armed bandits for nothing."

She laughed and fed another coin into her machine. "Ain't that the Lord's own truth. Still, a body can't help but try, now can they?"

She pulled the handle and hit three cherries. Five coins began to clank against the bin.

"Praise the Lord," she said, raking in her winnings. "And it's about time too."

Nick laughed. Then, as though some sixth sense of his was working overtime, he glanced over his shoulder and saw Jane, bundled up in her heavy wool coat, walking purposefully across the casino toward the main exit. She looked determined, committed to a mission that no one, including *el Diablo* himself, could have possibly kept her from fulfilling.

Yet she was still beautiful enough to turn every rational thought Nick had inside his head completely asunder with the gentle sway of her hips.

He stared at her for a moment, wanting to approach her, knowing that he needed to persuade her to change her mind about their partnership—knowing that she could compromise his own investigation if he didn't find some way to monitor hers—yet he didn't move.

The truth was he was too afraid that she might just scowl at him, then head off in the opposite direction as fast as those long legs of hers could carry her. He didn't think his bruised ego could withstand another direct hit just then.

As though her own sixth sense was pulling the

same double shift as his, Jane glanced in his direction and slowed to a stop. Rather than turn away, though, she started to walk toward him.

Praise the Lord, indeed.

Nick leaned over and slipped his bucket of coins in front of the woman seated next to him.

"It looks like my luck may be changing, *mi amor*," he said.

"Why, thank you, sugar," she murmured. "I think mine is too."

She fished into his bucket, grabbed a coin, then dropped it into the slot machine and pulled its handle as he rose to his feet and started to walk toward Jane.

Seconds later, the jackpot alarm on the top of the woman's machine began to sound, and dozens of coins started to hit the basin. He heard her let out a whoop of excitement along with another hallelujah, but he didn't look back.

The only thing Nick could see, the only thing he cared about seeing, was Jane.

They met next to a hand-carved staircase that led up to the second level of the casino. He decided that she looked even better close up than she had from across the room. Her face was slightly flushed and her eyes had deepened in color to the vibrantly alive green of a Mississippi spring. A few strands of her hair were dangling down along the curve of her cheek.

More than anything he wanted to reach over and smooth her hair back into place, to slide his fingers along the curve of her jaw, feel the warmth of her skin beneath his fingertips, but he fought hard against the impulse.

So he just gave her a smile instead. "Hi."

"Hi," she murmured back.

Her voice was still the same smoky contralto of his fantasies, and it still sent the same sensual shiver sliding down his spine.

Maybe even more so than usual this time.

Jane shoved her hands into the pockets of her coat and glanced around her.

"I'm glad I finally caught up with you," she said. "I must have spent a good fifteen minutes combing the casino, trying to find you. I searched all the roulette wheels and the poker tables, but I never thought to check the slot machines."

"You've been looking for me?" he asked, feeling surprised but no less pleased by the discovery.

"Yeah," she said. "Nick, we need to talk about reinstating our partnership . . . that is, if you're still interested."

Her expression was guarded, difficult to read.

He smiled again. "Oh, I'm still interested, Janie . . . but I'm surprised that you are, considering how you ran out on me last night."

Her flush started to deepen, and she glanced away. "Yeah, well, that was then."

"And this is now."

He regarded her for a moment longer, then shrugged.

"Like I said, I'm still interested in forming a

partnership. In fact, I've been following through on your theory about a possible connection between the games and the defective video recorder. You'll be happy to know it was right on target."

"I kind of figured it would be."

A middle-aged couple moved past them and started up the stairs. Nick took a step closer to Jane.

"Ah, look," he said. "Do you want to go somewhere so we can discuss our strategy? Maybe grab a cup of coffee or some lunch?"

"Either is fine with me."

His gaze dropped, and he saw the feather boa trim of her uniform peeking out from her coat. He frowned.

"Aren't . . . you supposed to be on duty right now?" he asked.

"Yeah," she said dryly. "But it's okay. Thanks to Tidwell, I no longer work as a cocktail waitress. I've been temporarily reassigned to human resources."

She slipped her hand into the crook of his arm and led him toward one of the casino's cocktail lounges across the room. The soft scent of lilacs danced around him, fogging his brain.

It made him feel as though he'd downed one too many tequila shooters when he'd had little more than coffee and club soda all morning.

"You spoke with Tidwell?" he asked.

He told himself to concentrate on what she was saying, that something had obviously happened in Tidwell's office to bring about her change of heart.

But the emotions tumbling through Nick from

the warm pressure of her fingers on his arm kept distracting him.

"Oh, yeah," she said.

"About last night?"

"Oh, yeah."

"So what happened?" he asked.

A pit boss walked past and gave them a curious look. Jane frowned and stopped just outside the door to the cocktail lounge.

"We probably shouldn't do this here," she murmured. She turned and tugged on his arm. "There's a coffee shop back onshore. Let's go there instead."

Again he shrugged. "Fine with me. But why all this cloak-and-dagger nonsense?" He cast her a speculative look out of the corner of his eye. "Just what did Tidwell say to you, anyway? And what do you mean that he's reassigned you to human resources?"

"I'll explain later."

She led him toward the exit. They made a quick stop at the courtesy bay where Nick retrieved his coat. He shrugged it on, then followed Jane outside.

The sky was gray and overcast, and a definite January chill hung in the air. Nick glanced toward the west and flipped up the collar on his coat. A slow-moving barge with a tarp-covered load was traveling down the Yazoo canal toward the Mississippi River, probably headed for New Orleans. A car horn blared from the casino's parking lot onshore. Then the sounds of laughter, of raucous language, floated up to them from the *Vicksburg Lady*'s dock where a boisterous party of five were coming aboard.

"The coffee shop's located between my motel and the Benedict Inn," Jane said. Her breath came out in a puff of white air.

Then, without waiting for an answer, she turned and headed toward the gangplank with a clatter of her high heels against the weathered wood.

"Do you want to tell me what this is all about, *cara*?" he asked, frowning again as he fell into step beside her. "I mean, exactly what did Tidwell say to you this morning? Did he suspect that we—?"

"Not now," she said, cutting him off. "I don't want to discuss this here."

The new arrivals walked past them, still laughing and looking as though they'd all had an early start on happy hour.

Nick fell silent and followed Jane down the gangplank toward the dock. He had dozens of questions that clamored for answers, but he doubted if she'd help him out with any of them until they were safely off the riverboat.

A short time later, they walked into Miss Penny's Diner where they were shown to a booth next to a large picture window by a bored-looking blond waitress in her early twenties.

Jane peeled off her coat, tossed it on the red vinyl seat next to her, and slid in to the booth. Nick did the same, taking the seat across from her. After pouring them a couple of cups of coffee and handing them their menus, the waitress left.

Jane reached for the artificial sweetener and poured a packet into her coffee.

Nick watched her stir the coffee, then tap her spoon gently against the rim of her cup.

"Okay, so we're in the coffee shop," he said quietly. "You even have your coffee. Now, will you please tell me what the hell happened back in Tidwell's office before I go completely out of my mind with worry?"

"Relax," she said, and took a tentative sip of her coffee. "I'll be happy to fill you in on all the gory details."

"Tidwell didn't fire you, did he?" he went on before she could elaborate. "Or punish you by giving you some desk job that'll interfere in your investigation of that runaway teenager? Because if he did, I can talk to him, flex a little muscle."

He reached for a packet of artificial sweetener and the creamer and began to add both to his coffee.

"As long as he thinks he's going to fleece me in our poker game, the man is going to want to keep me happy," he added.

She smiled and cradled her coffee cup in her hands. The diner's heating unit switched on, and a blast of forced heat blew down from the ceiling vent directly above their table. The feather boa trim of her uniform began to flutter, drawing his attention momentarily to her cleavage . . . and to the gentle curve of her breasts being hugged by the black nylon fabric of her dress.

He swallowed hard and forced his gaze back up to her face.

"Funny," she said. "You know that's just what Tidwell told me right before he gave me my new assignment . . . that he wants to keep you happy."

"Oh?" he asked, feeling as though their booth in the coffee shop had suddenly turned into a hundred-and-ten-degree sauna.

She set her coffee cup down on the table. "In fact, he's appointed me as your personal escort for the duration of your stay in Vicksburg."

He chuckled softly. "So *that's* what happened. Hell, *cara*, from the way you were sounding back at the casino, I was beginning to think that he was forcing you into white slavery or something."

"Yeah, well, that's close."

He raised his eyebrows.

"My new responsibilities," she said, "my *only* responsibilities, are to keep you content until the big game . . . and according to Tidwell, I'm to do whatever it takes to accomplish it."

"Anything?" he asked, intrigued. He leaned toward her.

"Yeah, anything . . . but don't get any funny ideas, Romeo. Our renewed partnership is going to be strictly platonic."

He reached for her hand. Despite having held the coffee cup, it felt chilled to the bone.

"Are you sure that's the way you want it to be?" he asked. "Having our . . . partnership . . . remain strictly platonic, I mean?"

He slowly stroked her wrist, feeling the pulse begin to flutter beneath his fingertips, feeling his own heart rate begin to escalate in response to hers.

"Of course, I'm sure," she said.

Her voice sounded breathless, as though it were colored by the same sensual heat blanketing him.

"All I'm interested in right now is shutting down the *Lady*," she added. "Besides, you're not even my type. I keep telling you that I don't like gamblers. I never have."

"And I keep telling *you* that I'm not addicted to the adrenaline rush of the game," he reminded her. "I never have been."

He smiled. "But all that doesn't really matter right now anyway," he said. "Your dislike of gamblers . . . casinos. You see, I'm finding it hard to believe you when you say that the only thing you're interested in is our investigation. Damn hard, in fact."

He linked their hands together, palm pressed to palm, fingers interlocked with fingers. He was amazed at how perfectly they seemed to fit.

It was almost as perfectly as her body had fit against his the night before.

"Because . . . when we were in the surveillance room lounge," he went on huskily. "When we were putting on our little performance for those guards . . . I could have sworn that you wanted our relationship to become more . . . personal."

"Then you were as taken in by my performance as Fitzpatrick and Landon were."

"Hmm. Nice try, but I don't think so. Not even Greta Garbo was that good of an actress."

She blushed. "I think you're imagining things."

"Am I?"

He took a deep breath and slowly exhaled, giving her hand a gentle squeeze. "*¡Válgame Dios, querida!*" he whispered softly. "Maybe you are a *bruja* sent here by the devil to steal my soul . . . because when you kiss me, I swear I can feel it start to slip away."

"That's ridiculous."

She twisted her hand and slipped it out of his grasp. "I think your ego's beginning to make your vision go hazy on you again," she said. "What happened last night . . . our kiss . . . it was just an act, Nick, something to get us out of a desperate situation and nothing more. Besides, the whole damn charade was your idea, or don't you remember that?"

She reached for her cup of coffee with both hands, as though the simple task of holding a piece of china couldn't be accomplished with just one. She took a long swallow.

"Oh, I remember," he told her.

How could he possibly forget? The memory of her kiss was burned into his psyche where it would likely haunt him forever.

"The way you touched my face," he said. "The way you shuddered against me . . . It was a great performance, but like I keep telling you, you can't fake that kind of a response, Janie, just as I can't keep denying to myself that I feel the same attraction for you."

He settled back in his seat with a crunch of well-used vinyl and gave her another grin.

"So what do you propose that we do about our little dilemma, *cara*? How are we to handle what we feel for each other?"

He lifted his coffee cup and took a sip.

"And please don't say that we're going to simply ignore our hearts and our bodies," he added huskily, paraphrasing her comment to him of some twelve hours before. "After all, we've tried that once and it didn't seem to work all that well."

She stared at him. "I suppose that you have the perfect solution for us, though," she said quietly.

"Oh, absolutely," he said.

"And it is?"

He shrugged. "I think we should surrender to our feelings and see where they lead us."

Which for him, unfortunately, could be straight to hell.

He sighed. It was probably a little late to be worrying about that, he thought, feeling his body begin to tighten, grow hard. Much too late.

SIX

Jane held his gaze for a moment, all too aware of the sexual energy pulsating between them.

She was all too aware of her body hungering for his touch . . . all too aware of the want for him that was surging through her bloodstream with the speed and destructive force of a swollen river through unprotected farmland.

This wasn't like her, dammit, she thought, trying to regain control. She didn't get swept away by her emotions the way her sister Kat did—nor had Jane ever gone absolutely gaga over a man before, which was something her sister seemed to do on a fairly regular basis. No, Jane was the *logical* one of the two Steele sisters.

She was the one who'd played surrogate mom from the time she was six, always making sure her younger sister said her prayers before bedtime and didn't forget to brush after meals. Jane was the dependable one, the practical one, the one who never, ever, did anything that could even remotely be considered impulsive.

Only now, it seemed that Jane was the one in dire need of some of that levelheaded advice she used to dispense to her sister. Because staring in Nick's sexy dark eyes, feeling the bone-and-sinew-melting heat of his twin-dimpled smile wash over her . . . well, it made her need him more than she did her next breath.

The desire was so acute, the passion so overwhelming, it was all she could do not to reach across the table, grab him by the lapels of his black wool jacket, and pull him toward her for a soul-shattering kiss that would probably get them both thrown into the Warren County jail on a morals charge before she'd finished with him.

"Nick, I . . ."

She took a deep breath and started again.

"I think that giving in to whatever it is you believe we feel for each other would be a mistake."

His grin only seemed to grow wider. "Now which one of us are you hoping to convince with that statement, *cara*? Me . . . or you?"

She flushed and set her coffee cup back down on the table.

"Maybe both of us," she said. "Hell, we both seem to have forgotten the reason we're together right now. We need to discuss Tidwell, formulate our strategy. Not discuss some fantasy of yours."

"I agree. Now isn't the time or place to discuss my fantasies."

The way he said the word *fantasies* made her flush intensify until she was certain that her face must match the scarlet trim of her saloon girl outfit.

"Besides, right now, I'm more concerned with what you're thinking," he said.

He placed his elbows on the table and leaned toward her. He wore another collarless silk shirt under his jacket. This one was a pale gray that stretched tautly across his firm, hard chest, almost molding itself to his well-defined muscles.

"Talk to me, Janie," he urged softly. "Are you afraid of what might happen if you give in to what you're feeling for me?"

Sweet heaven, she thought. Now the man was reading her thoughts as well.

"Of course not," she said, hoping her lie sounded convincing. "Because nothing is going to happen between us. Nothing at all."

Those twin dimples of his began to flash again. "*Cara*, something already *is* happening between us, or haven't you been paying attention to the messages that your heart and your body have been sending to your brain for some time now?"

"I . . ."

She felt as if she were drowning in a sea of sweet emotion. If she didn't regain control of the conversation, if she didn't put an end to this lunacy soon, she just might . . .

"So, have ya'll figured out what you want?"

The question came from their waitress, who seemed to have miraculously appeared at their table without a sound just when Jane needed her the most.

Jane let out a sigh of relief, thanking Providence for her brief reprieve, and leaned back against her seat. Nick, however, only grinned and handed the waitress his untouched menu.

"We both know what we want, all right," he said. "Unfortunately, one of us is still in denial."

Jane scowled. "Just bring us a couple of your lunch specials," she said, handing over her menu. "And a cold shower for my friend here, if you have one."

Nick laughed.

The sound was full and rich and so robustly male, it sent tingling sensations shooting through her lower abdomen that made her want to shiver.

The waitress looked from Jane to Nick, then grinned and slipped her pen back into the pocket of her uniform.

"A couple of chicken salad sandwiches and curly fries coming up," she said. "But I'd forget about that cold shower if I were you, honey . . . your boyfriend's kind of cute. I say go for it." Then she turned and left.

Looking overly pleased with himself, Nick leaned back in his seat and took a sip of coffee. "So what do you say, *cara*?" he teased. "Do you want to 'go for it,' as the lady suggests?"

"Dammit, Nick, this isn't a game."

He immediately sombered. "So why do you keep wanting to play one? *Dios*, Janie!" he said, leaning toward her. "I honestly don't understand why you won't admit that you want me as much as I do you. We're both adults. We're both single. What's the problem?"

"The problem is I'm working on a case. I don't have time to get involved with anyone right now. And even if I did . . ." She shook her head and took a deep breath. "Even if I did, how can I let myself get involved with a man that I know so damned little about?"

He held her gaze for a long while. "Fair enough," he said quietly. "So what do you want to know about me?"

She shrugged. "I don't know."

He could start with the important things, she thought, like why she couldn't stop thinking about him, or why the touch of his hand against hers seemed to short-circuit her brain, making her hormones completely run amok.

"Well, I'm single," he said. "Divorced, actually. No kids."

"Irreconcilable differences?" she asked.

He smiled. "Something like that. I spent a little too much time at work. Amber spent a little too much time at play. Living in Vegas can wreak hell with a marriage." He shrugged. "As for the rest of my vital statistics . . ."

He drained the coffee from his cup and set it back on the table.

"I'm thirty-four," he said. "I was born in Las Vegas, which is where I grew up with two sisters and a brother, all younger. I have an MBA from Harvard."

Harvard MBA?

She took a sip of her coffee and tried to process the new information. It didn't quite track with what she knew about professional gamblers, but then, the more time she spent with Nick, the less she truly believed that he was one.

"Until recently, I've been working in the family business," he said.

"Oh?" she asked, running the tip of her finger along the rim of her coffee cup. "What kind of business does your family have?"

He shrugged. "It's . . . a little hard to explain."

Her gaze locked with his. "Try."

A few seconds passed.

He sighed. "We run what you might call a service-oriented company. It's been around for eight generations now, in one form or another. We also manage a series of . . . investments . . . throughout the country. Mostly Nevada, but we've recently expanded into the South. New Orleans, Memphis, including a venture here in Mississippi. It's all actually pretty boring, though . . . for me anyway," he added wryly. "That's why I'm ready to strike out on my own."

"As a professional gambler?" she asked, still trying to tie together all the loose pieces of information that she had about him so she could form a complete picture.

"Not even close," he told her. "I want to buy a ranch, raise quarter horses. I came to Mississippi to look at some property."

She stared at him. "Quarter horses?" she repeated, not sure that she had heard him correctly.

"Yeah. Running a ranch has been a pipe dream of mine since college. I had a roommate from Mississippi whose family owned a place in Oxford. I went home with him one weekend. Three days were about all it took to get me hooked. The green trees, the fresh air, the horses . . . I knew that one day I'd be back."

"So why did you wait so long to do it?"

He shrugged. "I was young, still wasn't all that sure what I wanted to do with my life. Besides, other commitments, like the family business, kept getting in the way. Now, I'm older and my younger siblings are ready to take over. Luckily for us all, they like the business a lot more than I do. I guess they have my father's passion for it."

He smiled. "Sometimes I think that I must have taken after my mother's side of the family. One of my maternal great-grandparents was a *caballero* who used to work on a ranchero in old California. They tell me I even look a little like him."

She reached for her coffee and finished it off, trying not to think about a Wild West version of Nick Valdez, complete with silver belt buckle, leather chaps, and a black cowboy hat worn low over his brow.

It was no use, she decided. The unbearably erotic image was already firing her imagination into near meltdown.

"So, there you have it," he said, giving her another smile that made her pulse start to soar. "My life story condensed into a *Reader's Digest* version. Do you feel you know me a little better now?"

"I suppose," she said.

Actually, she felt more confused about him than ever before—and more confused about her own feelings for him.

"I do have one question," she said, deciding to eliminate a little of that confusion and redraw their professional boundaries in one fell swoop. "Just where am I supposed to fit in with all this?"

He looked puzzled. "Where are you supposed to *fit*? I don't follow you."

"I mean, you keep telling me that I shouldn't run from what I feel for you. Then you tell me that you're ready to pursue a lifelong dream of buying a horse ranch, which I think is great, but . . . but you haven't said anything at all about looking for someone to share that new life with you."

She met his gaze head-on. "I guess I'm asking you what, exactly, are you expecting will happen if I say I want to . . . well, 'go for it'?"

He grinned. "I'm hoping that we'll have several hours of mutually satisfying pleasure . . . and if we're lucky, maybe several hours more."

She blushed. "I mean, are we talking about a roll beneath the sheets or something that might lead to a long-term commitment? Do you want to use me for a couple of days or love me for a lifetime? Which is it?"

Now it was his turn to turn a little red. Her questions seemed to have taken him off guard.

Good, she thought. They were supposed to.

"*Cara* . . . I think it's a little too soon to be talking about lifetime commitments, don't you?"

"But not soon enough for us to be talking about having sex?"

"Considering the attraction that we have for each other . . ." He shrugged.

"But I don't have flings, Nick," she said softly. "I'm not a casual kind of person; sex isn't a casual kind of thing for me."

"I can appreciate that," he said, keeping his gaze locked with hers. "But I'm nowhere near ready to start thinking about any kind of a commitment—short, long, or somewhere in between. Hell, the ranch is going to take all of my time and energy to get it started, and I learned my lesson the hard way about trying to juggle a relationship and work. Maybe in a year or so—"

"But we're not talking about what will or won't happen in a year or so," she said, cutting him off. "We're talking about right now. And for right now, you want to have an affair and I don't. That's why we have to be sensible about our . . . attraction . . . for each other. Our partnership needs to remain platonic. Agreed?"

He scowled. "Janie, I . . ."

Before he could respond further, the waitress arrived with their food and a refill of coffee. Nick sighed and slumped back in his seat, as though he were accepting defeat.

"Yeah, I agree," he murmured once the waitress was gone. Then he reached for his napkin, which he spread across his lap. "The partnership will remain platonic."

"Thank you," Jane said, and reached for her own napkin.

She told herself that he'd given her the right answer, that she should be able to relax now and concentrate on the case. Only problem was Jane didn't believe him for a single, solitary moment.

She shot him a surreptitious look as he added a piece of sliced tomato and lettuce to his sandwich. She felt a rush of heat wash over her as her gaze slid down his broad, muscular chest one more time.

Then, again, how could she believe him?

She didn't even believe it herself.

Deciding it was pointless to continue arguing his case with Jane—mostly because he knew that she was right, much as his libido wished she wasn't—Nick redirected their conversation during lunch to the topic of how they should handle Tidwell.

They agreed that the upcoming private poker game was still their best bet of obtaining uncontrovertible proof of the nasty little scam Tidwell had going. They also agreed that, with the help of Jane's pals, the former-jewel-thieves-turned-security-experts, they would rig a surveillance camera in the room where the game would be played so they could capture all of that nastiness on videotape. Assuming, of course, that Nick was able to weasel the information about its location out of Tidwell beforehand.

In the meantime, they would attempt to identify which games on board ship were fixed. Thus far, they had three definites, all linked to the monitor marked *Main Room*, *View 11*. They would check out the two remaining video feed sources, a blackjack table and another row of slot machines, to see if they were rigged as well. If so, they had two choices. First was to investigate the video recorders in the other two surveillance rooms for signs of tampering. Fat chance, Nick thought, considering what had happened the last time they tried it. The second and more feasible, yet time-consuming, possibility was to conduct a systematic search through the casino for signs of rigged games.

Either way, they had a lot of work ahead of them. And they would probably have to do that work while being closely monitored by Tidwell, who'd more than likely want to make certain that Jane was following his edict to keep Nick "happy." Which Jane would have to appear to do whenever they were in public if they were to maintain their cover.

So, for the next hour, Nick and Jane talked and schemed and planned until they'd agreed on nearly every detail of their sting. Yet, through all the talking and scheming and planning, Nick's gaze kept darting toward Jane.

He seemed to notice a lot of little things about her now, like the way she had of tilting her head to one side when she was thinking something through, or the way she had of curling her lips into the cutest scowl he'd ever seen whenever something annoyed her.

Soon, Nick wasn't listening to what Jane said with quite the same attention as he had before. Instead, his thoughts were drifting to memories of their kiss back in the surveillance room lounge, to things like the taste of her mouth, or the feel of her body against his, or the hunger that grew inside him from her touch.

It was a hunger for more than just her body—although he tried his damnedest to ignore that part—which made it a hunger that he knew he couldn't satisfy. Not now. Probably not ever.

He was only looking for a mutually satisfying, no-strings-attached kind of romantic romp for the few days he'd be in Vicksburg. Jane was looking for an emotional commitment, a future, some kind of happily-ever-after fairy tale. It wasn't that he didn't understand her feeling the way she did; it was just that he wasn't the man to make that happen for her.

Hell, even if he bought that property outside Jackson and wanted to start thinking about something long-term, they still had a major obstacle between them. He was a Benedict. And Jane had made her feelings about casinos and the people who owned them only too clear.

Nick sighed. Yeah, he wanted her, and thinking about her was driving him *loco rematado*, but there was no relief to be found. Any way he rolled the dice, he still crapped out where she was concerned.

So he'd have to forget her. Simple as that.

Two days later, Nick decided that he had been overly optimistic about his ability to control his baser instincts around Jane.

He was gliding her across the crowded dance floor of the Benedict Inn's cocktail lounge and wondering just how in the hell he could have made such an asinine agreement to keep their relationship strictly platonic in the first place.

It felt so good drifting along to the music, holding her right hand close to his chest next to his heart, feeling the heat from the fingers of her left as they pressed gently against his neck. It felt so natural having her cheek resting against his shoulder, with the top of her head brushing his chin. It felt so right the way their bodies moved together as one, as though they'd danced this way for years. Holding her, having her hold him . . . It was like being lost in a dream.

Maybe that was his problem, Nick thought with a wry smile. He was lost in a dream, caught up in a fantasy when he knew damn good and well that dancing with Jane was supposed to be little more than another faux lovers' performance for Tidwell, who was watching them both from the other side of the room in between blowing puffs of cigar smoke at his unamused-looking girlfriend.

Nick took a deep breath, trying to concentrate on something else, anything else, trying with all his might not to think about how good and natural and right it felt to hold Jane.

He didn't quite succeed.

Amazing, he thought. Some thirty minutes earlier, he had been in complete control . . . or at least he thought he'd been. He had been sitting back in his chair, sipping a club soda and discussing the next phase of the sting with Jane. True, he'd been enjoying the way her short emerald-green skirt rode high along her tanned thighs, but he'd felt oh-so-proud of himself for being able to keep his libido firmly in check.

He had even been toying with the idea of telling Jane that she worked too damn much, that she should kick back a little, have some fun, maybe share a dance or three with him—in the spirit of their strictly platonic relationship, of course. After all, in the few days that he'd known her, she had always seemed to be doing something, either following up a lead in their own investigation or quietly asking around about the missing Traynor girl.

He figured Jane deserved a break. He figured he deserved a break.

He realized it probably wouldn't be wise for him to listen to any of his errant thoughts—nor would it be all that wise for him to examine his real reasons for wanting to get Jane out on that dance floor—then Nick had decided to call it a night.

That's about the time Tidwell and his girl-friend—who hadn't looked all that happy even then—had strolled into the cocktail lounge and taken a table directly within eyesight of theirs. Tidwell sent over a magnum of champagne—Moët & Chandon, yet—to Nick's table with the casino's compliments, along with a message that the poker game would be held that Sunday afternoon at six in a private room on the second level of the *Lady*.

Not wanting to blow their cover, or waste good champagne, Nick and Jane had drunk some of the sparkling wine. Then they'd moved their chairs closer together until their knees brushed and they could pretend to be gazing longingly into each other's eyes. They'd started to hold hands and make small talk. And he'd started to think he would go clean out of his skull from wanting to lean over and kiss her until neither one of them could breathe or move or talk.

Then Jane had suggested they dance.

And the trouble had really started.

The fast songs that the house band had been playing before Nick escorted Jane to the crowded dance floor had inexplicably changed to a series of bluesy standards guaranteed to inspire even the most spiritually minded couple to thoughts of erotic delight.

Nick had never been accused of being all that spiritually minded to begin with.

"Is he still watching us?" Jane murmured, not lifting her head from his shoulder.

"Probably," he murmured back. "Either that, or he's having another argument with Barbara. But who cares?"

She was quiet for a moment. They continued to drift to the music.

"I . . . don't . . . think I like that tone in your voice, *partner*," she told him finally.

Too bad, he thought, because he liked the tone of hers. It was soft and warm and breathless. He felt his body begin to tighten.

He thought about planting a soft kiss along the curve of her even softer earlobe. He would have done it, too, except he knew that a quick kiss would likely lead to a gentle nuzzle . . . and that gentle nuzzle would lead to his tracing the tip of his tongue along the ridge of her ear . . . and that exploratory journey of his tongue along her ear would lead to . . .

"You're not getting any of those funny ideas of yours again, are you?" she asked.

He smiled, wondering when she had turned psychic on him, and closed his eyes. Then he rubbed his chin lightly over the top of her head, loving the way her soft hair felt against his skin.

"What kind of funny ideas are you talking about, *cara?*" he asked.

"The kind you get when you let your imagination run away with you. The kind where you forget that this is all just make-believe. The kind where—"

"Shh," he told her, pulling her closer. "Your voice of reason is trying to drown out the whisper of my runaway imagination."

"Very funny."

"Besides," he went on, "Tidwell is expecting to see a man feeling completely *enamorado* over a woman, which is an easy thing to do where you are concerned, *cara*. Damn easy."

"Nick, I . . ." He felt her body tense. "Don't," she said.

Her voice sounded a little huskier than normal. He opened his eyes and raised his head. Her cheeks looked flushed.

He felt his abdominal muscles tighten. He told himself that he should stop now while he was still ahead on points, but he couldn't seem to help himself. It was as though his ego wouldn't let him get any peace until it was satisfied that she wanted him as much as he did her.

"You do like dancing with me, don't you?" he asked. "Or would admitting that you like this be a breach of your sacred oath to remain sensible at all times . . . even about matters of the heart?"

"This isn't about a matter of the heart," she muttered dryly. "It's about our overly stimulated hormones."

"Is it?"

"Of course it is! Besides, somebody has to remain sensible about what we feel for each other before we end up making a mistake that I'll probably regret. And, yes, that someone is me because I'm always the sensible one. *And* the practical one. *And* the dependable one."

He smiled. "You make it sound like you don't have a choice in what you are."

"I don't."

"Wrong," he told her, sliding his face against hers, feeling the flush of her cheek warm his skin. "We always have a choice. Sometimes we get lucky and make the right one. Sometimes we screw up. But we always have a choice, Janie. Always."

Hell, he'd even had a choice about leveling with her about his being a Benedict. First, he'd decided not to tell her because he wasn't sure that he could trust her with the information. Then time had passed and he'd decided not to tell her for purely selfish reasons. He knew how she felt about casinos and didn't want to have her look at him with disgust when she found out he was the Chief Financial Officer for one of the largest family-owned gambling concerns in the country.

Retired Chief Financial Officer, he silently amended, although the subtle difference would probably be lost on Jane.

He tightened his hold on her waist again, feeling the soft cashmere of her bulky sweater bunch beneath his fingers. He knew that if he didn't tell her soon, she'd find out on her own, and she deserved better than that. Hell, the poker game was three days away. Provided their sting went according to plan, Nick would be exposing Tidwell's cheating to the authorities, at which time Nick knew he'd *have* to identify himself as a Benedict.

He felt her sigh. She slid her left hand up his shoulder to rest against his neck, lightly ruffling his hair with her fingertips in the process. Her touch was gentle yet powerful enough to make his breath catch in his throat and his knees feel suddenly weak. Then the subtle fragrance of lilacs rushed over him, filling his lungs and his heart and maybe even a bit of his soul with the softly sweet scent of her.

He closed his eyes. Heat started to race through his blood. He swallowed hard. Besides, she was wrong, he thought. This . . . what they felt for each other . . . wasn't just about hormones and sex. It wasn't just physical. It went deeper than that for him, so deep, it was beginning to scare him.

"So tell me, *cara*," he murmured, trying not to think about the fear, trying only to concentrate on the pleasure of holding her.

"What would you like to do if you weren't always so dependable and sensible and practical all the time?" he asked.

She was silent for a moment.

"I'd be more like my sister Kat, I guess," she said, stroking her fingers through his hair again, sending fire-tinged tremors shooting down his spine.

"A little wild," she went on. "A little crazy. I'd be someone who could go with her impulses, regardless of how insane they might sound . . . Only I'm not that kind of person. I never have been."

"But you wish you were, right?"

"Sometimes."

He moved his hand up her back, strumming his fingers along the soft fabric of her sweater, knowing all about wishes. He was wishing right then that they were alone . . . he was wishing that he were touching her bare skin instead of her clothes . . . he was wishing that he were thrusting himself deep inside her body, that he was feeling those long legs of hers hugging him tight.

He grew so hard just thinking about loving her that his body began to ache.

"Then why not just do it?" he asked huskily. "Why don't you go a little wild? Get a little crazy? With me. Right now."

She raised her head and met his gaze. Her eyes were no longer cool; they were infused with heat, the same heat racing through his blood.

His arousal began to strain against his trousers. He took a deep breath, then slowly exhaled.

"We could go crazy together," he whispered. "*Loco de amor*. Just for tonight. What do you think?"

"I think you're already *loco*."

He grinned. "Probably, but you're evading my

questions again. Do you want to spend the night making love with me or don't you?"

She stared at him for a heartbeat, then frowned. "Nick, I . . ."

She didn't have to finish the sentence for him to know what she was going to say. A punch straight to his gut probably wouldn't have hurt as much.

The music began to slow, then ended altogether. Silence reigned for a moment.

"We're going to take a short break now," the band's vocalist crooned into the microphone. "See ya'll back here in fifteen for the last set."

The dance floor began to clear until Nick and Jane were the only ones who remained. He sighed—*¡Dios, but he was a fool where this woman was concerned!*—and reluctantly released her. Then he glanced over at Tidwell's table and noticed that the casino manager was gone, long gone from the looks of it, since a new couple was now occupying the same seats, which only made Nick feel worse somehow.

"Look," he murmured. "About what I said . . . forget it. I am *loco* right now. I don't—"

"Yes." She spoke so softly that Nick almost had to strain to catch her words.

Surprised, he turned back to meet her gaze. In a fraction of an instant, the heat in her eyes had turned into a near raging inferno of need and want and desire. Her lips were open partially, her breathing seemed irregular, and she looked so damned beautiful, his hands itched to reach out and pull her back into his arms.

Yet he didn't move.

"Excuse me?" he murmured.

"I want to spend the night with you," she whispered. "I want to go crazy with you, absolutely *loco de amor*. I want to make love to you until neither one of us can move. I want it so bad that it's all I can think about, all I can dream about, all I seem to care about."

He forced himself to take another breath. "I . . . I feel the same way about you," he said. "*Cara*, from the moment we met, all I wanted to do was take you into my arms and—"

"Stop."

Her hand shook as she pushed back her hair. "You see, I want a lot of things I can't have. You . . . you're just another one." She took a deep breath. "You're like a chocolate cheesecake, more or less."

"I'm like a cheesecake?"

He tried to smile but couldn't quite manage it. His jaw felt as if it were frozen in place.

She nodded. "I know how good that cheesecake would taste. I know how good it would make me feel if I gave in and ate the whole thing in one sitting. But I also know how guilty I'd feel the next day if I did. I know how much I'd regret having given in to the temptation when I realize that those once pleasurable feelings had turned to pain . . .

and that the empty spot inside me that I'd thought was finally filled had gotten even larger."

She glanced down at the floor. "That's why I force myself to remain sensible and practical and levelheaded anytime I'm around cheesecakes." She looked back up and met his gaze. "It's also why I can't let myself spend the night with you."

"*Cara* . . . Janie . . ."

"I'm sorry."

She turned and hurried over to their table, stopping only long enough to grab her purse and coat before heading out the door without a backward look.

Nick stood on the dance floor for a while longer, first feeling numb, torn between wanting to run after her and knowing that he should let her go, then cursing himself for wanting a woman that he knew he couldn't let himself have.

He ran his hands through his hair, knowing in his heart why he continued to pursue her although he still wasn't ready to admit the truth. He shook his head, trying to clear it. He couldn't be in love with her, he told himself. He just couldn't be. He walked back to the table, picked up his coat, draped it across his arm, dropped a twenty on the table as a tip for their waitress, and continued toward the exit.

He passed through the doorway into the lobby at the same time Jane was about to rush back into the lounge.

He stopped. She stopped. Their gazes locked. Then she smiled.

"On the other hand . . ." She sounded breathless.

She moved toward him and glided both her hands up his chest to rest on his shoulders.

"I can probably live a lifetime without another taste of cheesecake. I don't think I can survive another minute without a taste of you."

She melted against him, all softness and womanly heat.

"Thank God," he whispered hoarsely, and pulled her closer. He didn't think he could survive another minute without a taste of her, either.

SEVEN

Jane had to kiss him.

It was an urge she had no control over; it was a need as powerful as the one for food and drink. She had to kiss him or else she'd likely go mad from the sheer, unadulterated want of him. So she sighed and wrapped her arms around him, pulling him closer, loving the masculine hardness of his body against hers, loving the comforting warmth of his hands on her waist.

Most of all, she was loving the hunger, the all-consuming need that was burning in his eyes. She knew it was a hunger and a need for her.

Only her.

She closed her eyes and brushed her lips over his, trying to replicate the flutter of angel wings that his kisses had always reminded her of, although the heat rising off his body felt like it would incinerate her if she remained in its white-hot flame for too long. Still, she traded a soft, sweet kiss with him, a single kiss that quickly led to two, and then three, and then four, all the while ignoring the snatches of conversations and snippets of laughter from the other guests walking across the lobby. This . . . holding Nick, kissing him . . . was all that mattered to her. But it wasn't enough.

Growing bolder, she licked the tip of her tongue over his lips until he sighed and opened for her. She slid her tongue past his parted teeth into his mouth and sought out his as though it were the most natural thing in the world for her to do.

He still tasted of the champagne he'd drunk earlier. It made her feel giddy, light-headed. Her heart started to pound. Her mouth went dry. She needed more.

Growing bolder still, she glided her tongue around his, caressing it the way that she wanted to caress his body . . . wanting to arouse him the way that their slow dancing had aroused her . . . promising them both with her kisses just how good it would be between them.

He moaned deep in his throat and cupped his hands around her face, returning her kisses with such fervor, yet with such unbearable gentleness, it threatened to seduce her very soul. Still, it wasn't enough. She needed to feel him shudder from her touch, needed to feel him lose himself in her the way that she felt lost in him.

She needed to make love to him for an hour, or a week, or maybe a decade or two.

She tripped her fingers up his neck, ruffling his hair, and moved closer to him until his erection pressed hard against her lower abdomen. Then she slowly rubbed herself against him like a cat who was demanding to be stroked, loving the heat and the hardness of him. She slid her tongue over his tongue, moving faster now, sucking him, massaging him, trying to use her body to communicate the yearnings of her heart.

She felt him shudder. *Wonderful*. Yet it still wasn't enough.

Nick moaned again, deeper this time, then gently pushed her away.

"*¡Dios, cara!*" he said huskily. "What are you trying to do to me? Drive me insane?"

Her eyes fluttered open. His face was flushed, his dark eyes smoldering from the same internal fire that consumed her. He raked a hand through his hair and glanced around him at the other people in the lobby but, again, Jane just ignored them.

Instead she smiled. "I would have thought that what I'm trying to do was obvious," she murmured, moving closer to him.

"Maybe too damned obvious, *bruja*."

His voice was rough, thick with emotion. She decided that she loved the way he sounded, so out of control. So under her control.

She reached up and touched his face. His skin burned as though from a fever. She stroked his cheek.

"If I were a *bruja*, I think I would cast a spell over your heart . . ."

"You already have, *querida*."

". . . Because I want you," she went on softly. "I want to make love to you. I want you to make love to me. Right this moment."

She brushed her lips over his and felt him shudder against her again.

"I thought that was what you wanted too," she said. She kissed the tip of his chin. "Or have you changed your mind about wanting to go *loco de amor* with me?"

He laughed, low and husky. "Oh, I want you, *mi amor*," he said, sounding breathless. "I just don't want to get arrested showing you how much, which I may do if you kiss me again."

As though on cue, a uniformed security officer walked past them, glowering disapproval.

Jane felt herself blush. She knew she was acting like a fool, behaving no better than Marybeth Traynor and her boyfriend at Daddy Traynor's country club party, yet Jane didn't care. She wanted Nick, needed him—heaven help her, but she probably loved him too!—even though logic and common sense told her that the most they could ever have would be a wildly glorious fling lasting maybe a week or two. A month if she was lucky. Even without the gambling issue—which she was fast realizing was no true issue at all—Nick had made it clear that he wasn't interested in anything even approaching long-term.

But logic couldn't compete with emotion. Her heart told her that he needed her as much as she did him. Her heart told her that, regardless of what he might have said to the contrary, he wanted more than simply a wildly glorious fling with her. He kissed her as though she were his, for now and for always. He looked at her as though she were a natural royal flush when all he'd been used to getting in the game were deuces and threes. Most of all, he touched her . . . oh, when he touched her, she felt as though her skin were too damned tight for her body, so tight that it was about to burst through its seams. For once in her life, dammit, she was going to give in to every hedonistic impulse that came her way.

"But I want to kiss you," she whispered, rubbing the pad of her thumb over his lips. "And I want to touch you . . . and I want to make love to you . . . right now."

He squeezed his eyes closed. *"Cara . . ."*

"So I guess we'd better get up to your room," she said, grabbing his hand. She started to lead him over to the row of elevators.

"Before we both get ourselves arrested," she added.

The ride up to the fourth floor seemed like the longest two and a half minutes of her life.

All Jane wanted to do, all she could think about doing, was reaching over and touching Nick, stroking her hands over his taut, muscular body, unbuttoning his shirt to rain kisses down his neck and chest, tasting his skin. But she restrained herself. For one thing, they weren't alone. Two cowboy-hat-clad men in their late forties, their spirits buoyed by a night spent gambling at one of the other riverboat casinos along the canal, were in the elevator with them.

Besides, Jane knew that once she started touching Nick, she would never, ever be able to stop. So she held her libidinous inclinations in check until they were safely inside his room.

"Would, ah, you like a drink?" he asked.

He tossed his room key onto the top of the television set, then dropped his coat onto one of the chairs. He looked nervous, suddenly unsure of himself while she had never felt more certain of anything in her entire life than she did of what she was feeling for him.

She smiled and slipped off her shoes. "I'm fine."

"Are you sure? Because I think there's some wine in the minirefrigerator, or I could call down to room service and order something. Coffee. A bottle of brandy, maybe. Whatever you want."

She shrugged out of her coat and moved toward him. "All I want, all I need, is you."

She tossed her coat onto the chair next to his, then grabbed him by the lapels of his jacket and pulled him to her until their bodies touched. She felt him tense for a moment, then he slid his hands around her waist to grasp her buttocks. His palms scorched through the heavy cotton of her short green skirt to singe her skin.

"You're all I need too," he said huskily.

A wave of heat rushed over her, making her knees go weak and her heart pound out of control. She tugged on his lapels, pulling him closer, then she kissed him. Not soft, sweet kisses this time. They were hard, fiery ones, more like the caresses of a demon than the gentle brush of angel wings. She moaned softly and thrust her tongue back into his mouth, needing to savor the intoxicatingly wonderful taste of him one more time.

He cupped her buttocks, then pulled her up to him until her hips were aligned with his and his erection rested between her thighs. He rocked her body against his for a moment, moving his hardness over her aching heat, again and again and again, teasing her, tormenting her with the feel of him against her, until a shudder racked her and her abdominal muscles began to spasm.

She broke the kiss and tightened her hold on his lapels until the tremor passed.

Sweet, sweet heaven.

"*Cara . . . mi amor.*"

His voice was soft and streaked with need. His breath felt warm against her neck.

He pulled her closer to him. "You feel so good," he murmured.

"So . . . do you."

"But . . . *¡Dios,* this is going to kill me!" He

brushed his cheek against hers and gave her a kiss on her ear. "Maybe we should slow down."

She laughed. *"Slow down?"*

He had to be joking. She wanted to feel more of him, wanted to taste more of him. She wanted to go *loco de amor* with his body in a way that she'd never wanted a man before.

"I'm serious," he whispered, and slowly pushed her away. "I think . . . I think we should stop. Just for a little while."

She reluctantly released his lapels and looked up to meet his gaze.

"You're beginning to sound the way I used to," she accused. "Sensible. Practical. Levelheaded."

He gave her a smile, but his dimples weren't winking at her this time.

"I have to be," he told her. "One of us has to remain sensible and practical and levelheaded at all times, if only to prevent us from doing anything that you'd end up regretting later . . . remember?"

She flushed. "I was wrong to say that."

She moved her hands under his jacket to touch him through his shirt, feeling the heat of his body rise up to scorch her fingertips.

"And the only regret I'll have is if we stop this," she told him.

She glided her hands down his body to stroke his chest and his abdomen, then lower still, sliding her hands over his thin leather belt to touch his arousal.

He drew a sharp breath and closed his eyes, surrendering himself to her.

"*¡Cara!*"

This . . . this was what she wanted, she realized with a flash of sudden insight. She wanted his total surrender, the knowledge that he was giving her both his body and a large piece of his soul to do with as she wished, he was giving all of himself to her in response to the simple touch of her hand against him.

Her heart thudded wildly. She felt as if she couldn't breathe.

Her hands trembled as she ran them between his thighs, feeling his strength, his heat, rush up and swamp her. She trailed her fingertips over his erection, teasing him, returning the torment, before gently cupping him with her palms. She hesitated for a moment, amazed that she had become so brazen, then she massaged him until he shuddered against her hands, whispering her name like a prayer.

"I can't wait to taste you," she whispered, increasing the tempo of her strokes. "I can't wait until you are locked inside me . . . hard and strong. I can't wait to feel you come inside me."

He muttered a curse in Spanish. Or maybe it was a prayer of thanksgiving. Either way, he shuddered again, then pushed her hands away.

"I . . . I can't wait, either," he said hoarsely. "But—*¡Dios, cara!*—if you keep touching me that way, if you keep talking to me like some *bruja* trying to steal my immortal soul . . ."

He drew a slow, deep breath, as though he were trying to regain his composure, then he gave a shaky laugh.

"If you don't stop, *mi amor*, we'll be over before we ever get started."

She smiled. "You make it sound as if we only get one shot at this. We could have all night together if you wanted."

And the next night if he wanted that, and the one after it too. Hell, if Nick asked her, she would gladly give him eternity.

"Exactly," he said. "We have all night. That's why I think we should slow down a little. Take our time. Besides, we . . . we need to talk."

She shook her head. "I don't want to talk. Unless it's to tell you all the wonderfully naughty things that I want to do to you."

His cheeks flushed. "Jane . . ."

"You used to call me Janie," she reminded him huskily. "Now it's back to plain old Jane."

"Beautiful, bewitching Jane," he corrected. "I've decided it's the sexiest name of all time. Besides, I thought you preferred Jane to Janie."

She shrugged. "From most people I do."

"But not from me?"

She shook her head and pulled off his jacket, which she dropped onto the chair on top of her coat.

No, from him she wanted Janie and *cara* and

querida and all the other silly little endearments in Spanish that he peppered their conversation with.

She fumbled with the buttons on his shirt and took a deep breath. He smelled so good, she thought. All musk and spice and man.

His hands slid over hers, stopping her.

"Janie . . . *mi amor* . . . we need to talk about this, about what we're doing before we get so caught up in our passion that we can't stop."

"But I don't want to stop," she said, then kissed his chin, pulling his body closer to her. "Not now . . . not ever."

"That's . . . what I'm afraid of," he murmured, gently pushing her away.

She regarded him for a moment. Hunger still burned in his eyes, so she knew he still wanted her, that he still needed this as much as she did. Yet she could feel his hesitation as acutely as she could his desire.

"Am I being too aggressive?" she asked, trying to figure out the reason for his reluctance. "You said that you wanted me to go crazy, totally *loco de amor*. But maybe you don't like having a woman take control during sex. Maybe you'd prefer to make all the moves."

"No . . . it's not that." He sighed. "I love having you take charge. I love your wickedness . . . your boldness. I love how you touch me . . . how you talk to me. It's perfect, *cara*. You're perfect."

"So what's the problem?"

She pushed him back onto the bed. He hit it

dead center. She dove in after him and started to undo his shirt buttons in earnest now.

"The problem . . ."

He took a deep breath and stilled her hands.

"The problem is us, or rather me," he said. "There are things about me that you don't know. Things that you may not like."

"It's okay," she said. "I know everything I need to know about you."

"But you don't," he said, releasing her hands. "There's one thing that you don't know, one question I've always evaded answering each time you bring it up because I didn't want to have you turn away from me in disgust."

He raked his hand through his hair and looked so miserable that she wanted to pull him into her arms and hold him forever.

"I know how you feel about people who make their living in the gambling business," he said. "I used to be . . . I mean, my family—"

"Don't," she said. "What you used to be doesn't matter. Nothing matters except what we feel for each other right now."

His gaze locked with hers. "Maybe it doesn't matter to you now. But what about tomorrow? What if you wake up and decide that you've made a terrible mistake? What if you realize that what I used to do for a living, who I am, really does matter to you? What then, *cara*?"

Better yet, she thought, what if she woke up tomorrow and discovered that what she believed was love shining so brightly in Nick's eyes was really only passion, a passion forever quelled by one night together?

She took a deep breath.

"Life, love . . . it's all about taking risks," she said, more for her own benefit than his. "Nothing comes with a guarantee. Absolutely nothing. We can calculate the odds, but we still have to make the leap on faith alone."

She leaned over and touched his face, feeling the warmth of his skin, the bristle of his five o'clock shadow, knowing that, with him, she would make any leap.

"But why am I telling you any of this?" she asked. "You're the gambler. You know more about taking risks than anyone."

"But that's just it. I'm not a—"

"Shh," she said, gliding her thumb over his lips, interrupting him. "It doesn't matter. I promise you, the only regret that I'll ever have is if we don't make love right here. Right now."

She let her thumb float down his lips to rest on his lightly stubbled chin. She decided that she loved the rustle of his baby whiskers against her hand.

She decided that she loved him.

He frowned. "But—"

"No but's. I want you . . . and unless I've been hallucinating for the past hour or so, I think you want me too."

He stared at her for a moment. Moaning softly, he slid his hands up her face to touch her hair. He wove his fingers through its strands, then gripped both sides of her head and held her fast.

"Oh, Janie, *mi amor*, I want you more than life," he said huskily.

Her stomach did a flip-flop.

"Then kiss me," she said. "Kiss me as if you never want to stop."

He smiled, dimples twinkling, and leaned into her. His eyes fluttered closed, then he brushed his lips over hers, once, twice, then a third time. She reached down for the opening of his shirt, gathered the loose folds into her hands, and pulled him closer. She opened her mouth and slid her tongue between his parted lips.

He moved his tongue alongside hers, pulling her deeper into his mouth, seducing her senses with the taste of him, tempting her soul with the erotic feel of his tongue dancing with hers.

The kiss grew, deepened until she realized that she'd have to modify her definition of the word *ecstasy* to include kissing Nick. She released her grip on his shirt and undid the rest of his buttons. Her hands shook as she pulled off his shirt, gliding it down his firm, smooth chest, tugging it off his strong, muscular arms. It was too much. She moaned and pulled away, reaching for his belt.

"Tell me what you want," he said hoarsely as she loosened his belt and undid his trouser zipper.

She let her gaze slide down his body, loving its heat and its hardness and the way that it had felt pressed against hers.

"That . . . all . . . depends, I guess," she said.

She drew her hands down his hips and legs, then grasped his left shoe.

"As a woman, I want your body."

"It's yours."

She pulled off the shoe and tossed it to the floor, then reached for the next one.

"As a *bruja*, I guess I'd want your soul," she said. "And maybe even your heart."

"They're already yours," he said without hesitation. "What else can I give you? Tell me what you want from me, and I swear, *cara*, I'll make it happen if I can."

She smiled. "You can give me this. You can give me tonight."

She peeled off his socks, then reached for his pants and began to tug them down his hips. He raised up on his elbows to give her easier access, but that was all he did to help. He seemed to understand without her having to ask that she needed to undress him.

"Are you sure that's all you want from me?" he asked. "Just tonight?"

She hesitated and almost told him the truth, that she was falling in love with him, that she *had* fallen in love with him, that she wanted tonight and every night thereafter. But she didn't.

"We'll start with tonight," she said.

She couldn't allow herself to dream any further than that.

"And for tonight," she went on, "I want you to let me go completely *loco de amor* with your body. I want you to let me act out my wildest fantasies with you."

She let the trousers slide to the floor next to his shoes, then ever so slowly slipped her fingers under the waistband of his boxers and gave the elastic a gentle tug. He shuddered.

"Agreed," he said.

His voice was layered throughout with a hunger that made her tremble.

"Provided that you allow me to act out a few of my fantasies concerning you," he added.

She smiled. "You've had fantasies about me?"

He moved his hand over her left thigh, pushing up the hem of her short skirt, making her skin tingle and burn from his touch.

"Since I was old enough to know what fantasies were," he said softly, reaching for the zipper on her skirt.

He started to tug it down, one slow, gentle inch at a time, until she felt as though her blood had turned to liquid fire, a fire that seemed to burn from her soul straight up through her skin. She trembled from its heat, trembled from its power.

"I've been dreaming of someone like you for that long," he went on, rolling her skirt down her hips, gliding it past her black silk panties, gently raking his nails over her as he moved down her stockingless thighs.

"I just didn't realize that it *was* you, Janie *mi*

amor," he went on, "until I heard you speak that first night at the poker table."

The heat was all around her now. It was scorching through her fingertips, blazing through her hair. It was everywhere he touched her. It was him.

She felt herself flush. "I . . . hope . . . I live up to the expectations of your fantasy," she said, feeling breathless.

She let him pull the skirt down her knees, shifting slightly so he could pull it off altogether. He dropped the skirt to the floor, then he helped her remove her bulky sweater, which he deposited next to the rest of their clothes.

"*Mi amor* . . . you've already exceeded my expectations," he said.

He slid his hands over her lacy black brassiere, stroking her breasts for a moment, making the fire inside her burn hotter, making her burn hotter. Then he gently tweaked her nipples through the lace between his thumb and forefinger, bombarding her senses with blasts of pure pleasure. She moaned and arched herself toward him.

"How did you know I loved black lace?" he murmured, sliding his hands around her back to unclasp her bra.

"I . . . a *bruja* knows all."

He laughed, low and deep. The sound stoked the fire inside her until she couldn't breathe because even the air itself was the heat of his touch.

"*Cara* . . . I do love the way you look in silk and lace," he murmured. His voice had acquired a lazy, dreamlike quality. "I'd love to dress you in every item of lingerie they sell. But only if you'd swear that you'd wear them for no one but me."

"There is no one but you."

He pressed his lips to her cleavage, then slowly raked his tongue over her skin, making it sizzle and burn. A spasm rocked her.

"Promise?" he asked.

She closed her eyes and leaned in to him. She slid her fingers through his hair and pulled him closer, needing him closer.

"I'd promise you anything," she said.

"Then would you promise me more than just tonight?" he asked softly. "Would you promise me tomorrow? And all the days that follow? Would you, Janie . . . *mi amor?*"

"I . . . thought you weren't interested in any long-term commitments."

"I wasn't until I met you."

He slowly slid the straps of her bra down her shoulders and off her arms, then dropped the brassiere over the side of the bed.

He sighed. "*¡Dios*, but you're beautiful!"

He palmed her breasts in his hands, touching her with all the heart and emotion that she could have ever asked him for. Words began to bubble up inside her. Again, she wanted to tell him that she loved him, she wanted to tell him about the power that he held over her . . . but, again, she held back. The risks were simply too high.

"Witch." He breathed the word against her

skin. "Do you have any idea how much I want you right now?"

He flicked his tongue over her right nipple, drawing it deep into his mouth, while continuing to stroke and caress her left breast with his hand. The fire coursing through her blood began to settle in her lower abdomen where it burned with a flame that could never be dampened.

She needed him. Now.

She stroked his chest. "Do you know how much I want you?"

He gave her a twin-dimpled smile. "Tell me."

She brushed her lips over his. "Let me show you instead . . . Besides, I still want my fantasy, Nick," she added huskily. "Will you let me have it?"

He took a deep breath. "I'm yours."

She slowly tugged his boxers down over his erection. He winced, but didn't try to help other than to raise his hips so that she could pull off his underwear.

She marveled at the naked perfection of him. He was all male, so glorious and pagan in his beauty that she reveled in her own femininity when she looked at him. She touched his face first, wanting to memorize its every curve and angle. Then she touched his neck, and his shoulders, and his chest, slowly gliding her hands over every warm, hard inch of him. She paused to trace a fingertip over his nipples, feeling them tighten into little buds beneath her. Then she kissed his chest, hitting the spot right above his heart.

His skin burned her lips just as the power of his need burned her soul. The rapid staccato rhythm of his heart, the rush of his blood through his veins, both filled her ears until soon that was all she could hear.

She moved her hands lower, past his navel, past his washboard-flat abdomen, down to the mass of soft dark curls surrounding his arousal. Relying more on instinct than experience, she caressed him with both hands. At first, her touch was uncertain—she'd never been so bold with a man before—but she quickly grew more confident as he began to moan.

Amazing, she thought.

She'd made love before but it had never been like this, all carnal heat and spiritual bliss. She had never wanted to please a man the way that she wanted to please Nick, either. Nor had she ever received such satisfaction from knowing that she was pleasing him.

His arousal felt like hot velvet between her hands. So hard, yet so soft. Before she realized what she was doing, she leaned down and kissed its tip.

He shuddered beneath her, murmuring her name.

That's when she decided to act out her wildest fantasy of all. She slowly took him into her mouth, gliding her hands down his shaft to caress him. He tasted of heat and of Nick, of love and of magic.

"*Janie . . . mi amor . . . mi corazón.*"

He said other things. Words she understood only with her heart. She slid her tongue around the hard length of him, loving the power and the control that he was letting her have over him.

She pulled her fingers back up his shaft, paused a moment, then moved them down him again, taking him farther inside her mouth, wanting to seduce his very soul the way he had seduced hers. A shudder rippled through him, yet she continued to pleasure him, using her tongue and her lips and her hands to caress him.

"Enough," he said, sounding as though he were drowning from their heat. "I . . . I'm too close. I can't hold back any longer."

"I don't want you to hold back."

He muttered another prayer—or was it a curse?—in Spanish and thrust his hips toward her as a spasm gripped him.

He *was* close, she thought, sliding her lips back over him. So close that she could feel the orgasm rumbling through him.

"*¡Cara!*"

Grabbing one of the pillows, he sat up and gently pushed her away, then tucked the pillow in front of his hips and gripped her shoulders as the release started to overtake him.

"Hold me," he said with a groan.

And she did.

She wrapped her arms around him and held him to her as he rode it out, whispering her name over and over, telling her how good she'd made him feel, telling her how badly he wanted to reciprocate the pleasure, telling her things that alternated between making her want to blush and making her want to take him again.

When the tremors stopped and he was finally still, she brushed back the perspiration-dampened hair along his forehead and gave him a soft kiss on his temple.

"Thank you," she murmured, feeling stronger and more adored than she had ever felt before in her life. "I really needed that."

Nick slowly raised his head to look at her.

Thank you?

He took a deep breath, held it, then slowly exhaled. Maybe Jane was one of *el Diablo's* angels, he thought in amazement. She made him burn hotter than Death Valley in the summertime, she made him lose hold of both his sanity and his self-control with the touch of her talented little hands and a sensuous kiss that still made him tremble, and yet here she was thanking *him* for the privilege.

"I think," he said, taking another deep breath. "I think I'm the one who's supposed to thank you."

She smiled. It was a soft smile, full of caring and honest emotion, and it fed his heart until he thought it would burst from her love.

"That was . . . incredible," she said.

"Beyond incredible," he told her, pulling her down with him on the bed until they lay side by side. He was silent for a moment, content with just holding her. "It's not that I mind solo flights," he went on, stroking her arm, "but why didn't we fly together?"

She kissed his shoulder. Her lips burned his skin. "We were fulfilling my fantasy, remember?"

He smiled, feeling the blood begin to race to his groin and that cord of tension start to wind tighter inside him. "Right." He sat up a little. "Now it's time for one of mine."

He slowly stroked his hands down her body, caressing her breasts, amazed at how they fit so perfectly into his palms, then he massaged her abdomen above the tiny wisp of silk that covered her hips. She *was* beautiful, he thought with an awareness that rocked his very soul. And she was his. All his.

All his, a cold voice inside his head reminded him darkly, until she found out that he was a Benedict.

No!

Nick squeezed his eyes closed, refusing to think about the unthinkable . . . and losing Jane's love and trust was unthinkable.

He sighed and opened his eyes, then slid his hand between her legs and started to touch her, needing the reassurance of her passion. He could feel her moist heat seeping through the silk to wet his fingers. He could also feel her hunger and her need. A soft moan slipped from her lips.

She slowly moved against him. "May . . . I tell you a secret?"

He smiled. "You can tell me anything."

He found her tightened nub of desire and began to stroke it through her panties with the pad of his thumb. Back and forth. Faster and harder.

"I . . ." She shuddered against his hand. "I really don't need all that much foreplay right now. I'm . . . past . . . ready."

He laughed, loving the huskiness of her voice, loving the way it was filled with an ache of longing for him, for his touch.

"But I need to make you go as *loco* as you've made me, *querida* . . . and you did promise me that we could act out my fantasy once we'd acted out yours."

She began to move her hips against his hand. "I . . . yes."

"So will you let me have my fantasy? Will you give me your body?"

Another tremor shook her. She drew a shaky breath, and her fingers shot out for the bedspread.

"Yes," she said with a rush of air.

"And will you give me your heart?" he asked, dropping his voice lower, intensifying his strokes. "Will you give me your soul if I were to ask for it?"

She gripped the bed linens in her fingers and squeezed them so tight, her knuckles began to turn white.

"They're . . . already yours," she said.

"Then will you give me your control?" he asked. "Will you give me your passion?"

"I . . ."

He brushed his lips against the flimsy silk of her panties, inhaling the musky scent of her. He raked his tongue across her until she gasped and arched her body to meet his mouth.

"Nick!"

Her moan seemed to be torn from her soul. He recognized the sound. It was a cry of joy, of absolute bliss at finally discovering the one thing you'd spent your entire life searching for. It was how his soul had rejoiced when Jane had first touched him.

He kissed her again through the silk, wetting his tongue over her again and again, gently sucking her through her panties, until she writhed with wild abandon beneath his mouth.

"Please," she said. "I need . . ."

"I know," he whispered back. "I need it too."

He slipped the panties down her hips and let them fall. He leaned over and fumbled with the top drawer of the nightstand. He yanked it open and removed a condom.

Seconds later, he parted her thighs and slid into her. Her heat surrounded him, stealing his breath, but he didn't need it because she was his breath. She was his life. Her muscles constricted around him, holding him tight. *¡Dios!* He moved against her, searching for their rhythm. He found it, lost himself in it, then lost himself in her. This was better than a dream, he thought. Better than a fantasy too. This was heaven.

Her hands tightened on his shoulders, her nails bit into his flesh, but he didn't mind the pain. She started to moan. He could feel her falling into her climax, and then he started to fall too.

Heaven, he thought again as his world started to explode.

"*Mi amor . . . mi corazón*," he whispered hoarsely against her ear.

Because she was his love and his heart.

"*Mi amor . . . mi . . . corazón*," she whispered back.

And his soul rejoiced.

EIGHT

Night slipped into day.

Nick awoke around nine. He lay there for a long while, not moving a muscle, just watching Jane sleep, marveling at the awesome beauty of her and content with feeling the warmth of her body curled into his. This—holding her, having her hold him—was the first true peace he'd ever known. He'd have gladly stayed there with her for the rest of his life if he could have, holding her tight, inhaling the scent of her skin and knowing in his soul that their hearts were beating as one.

Unfortunately, the odds weren't in his favor of that ever happening. He knew he was only living—and loving—on borrowed time. Soon, Jane would discover that he was a Benedict. While she might forgive him for withholding his true identity and the real reason for his being at the *Lady*, he doubted if she'd ever forgive him for lying to her.

And yet he was too afraid that he'd lose her if he told her the truth.

Nick sighed—when had things gotten so damned complicated? he wondered—and closed his eyes. Then he let Jane's steady, rhythmic breathing lull him into a prolonged state of inertia that didn't end until she started to stir some thirty minutes later.

He opened his eyes and smiled. "Good morning, *mi amor*," he murmured, leaning down to kiss her.

She stretched, and her eyes fluttered open. Then she gave him a smile that was so warm and loving, it made his heart start to sing.

"Good morning," she murmured back. Her voice was thick with sleep but still streaked with emotion.

And then it hit him. He loved her, more totally and unequivocally than he'd ever loved anyone before. He wanted to touch her, had to touch her or else he'd die from the need, so he reached over to stroke her face, amazed by its dewy fresh silkiness.

He was amazed by her, amazed by them.

Amazed by love.

"Any regrets?" he asked softly, pushing her hair off her forehead.

"Not a single one."

"Good."

It would have killed him if she'd said anything else.

"So, how do you feel?" he went on. "Did you sleep well?"

"Fishing for compliments so soon?" she teased.

"Absolutely."

She laughed. "In that case, I slept wonderfully, thank you, and I feel . . ."

"Yes?"

"Hungry." She started to smile.

"For me?" he asked, smiling back. He let his hand drop lower.

"No, for breakfast, silly."

She pushed away his hand and struggled into a sitting position, then tucked the sheet around her breasts.

"I'm starved for food," she went on. "Right now, I feel like I could eat—"

"A whole cheesecake?" he suggested.

She laughed. "Exactly."

"Me too."

He pushed down the sheet and palmed one of her breasts in his hand, then he rubbed his thumb over its nipple until it puckered into a tightened nub.

"Except I'm starved for you, *mi amor*," he said. "I'm starved for your passion, for your love."

"You're . . . making me blush."

"I love it when you blush."

He let his hand drop lower, skimming over her abdomen to the juncture of her thighs, where he ran his fingers through her silky dark curls.

"I love it almost as much as I love watching you come," he added huskily.

"I . . ." She shuddered against his hand. "Are you always so damned frisky in the morning?"

He grinned. "You'll have to spend the night with me a few more times to find out."

"Hmm. How many times do you figure it would take?"

"I don't know."

He kissed her shoulder, then the side of her neck. Her pulse fluttered wildly against his lips.

"What are you doing the rest of your life, *mi corazón?*" he asked.

"Careful," she said. "If you keep talking like that, I might begin to believe you're serious."

"But I am serious." He kissed her ear, then her cheek. "I want more than just one night with you, *cara* . . . I want forever . . . and from the way you make love, I think you want forever too."

"But—"

His lips captured hers, cutting off her protests. She tensed for a moment, then she moaned softly and opened for him. His tongue moved inside her mouth with practiced ease as her hands slowly migrated down his shoulders, touching him, caressing him.

He broke the kiss and started to nuzzle her ear as his thumb sought out the tiny nub of tension between her thighs. He began to massage her, gently at first, then increasing his tempo in response to her throaty murmurs of pleasure.

"Forever . . . does sound wonderful." She breathed the words against his hair. "Too bad we can't always get what we want."

"Oh, Janie, *mi amor*," he whispered back, increasing the intensity of his strokes. "But we can. If spending forever with me is what you want, I swear to God, I'll make it happen for us . . . because it's what I want too."

"I . . . oh, Nick!"

His name came out in a low, ragged moan. She arched her hips toward him, communicating the needs of both her body and her soul in a way that words never could. His fingers slid inside her. She was wet. Hot. Ready. His body ached to join with hers.

Smiling, he started to slow the rhythm of his strokes, teasing her now, loving the way she moved against his hand, loving the way she clutched at his shoulder and her eyes burned with raw need.

"*Mi corazón*," he whispered. "I'd like nothing better than to show you just how wonderful forever could be with me. We could start right now, in fact." He eased his hand away from her. "But of course, if you'd rather eat breakfast than make love . . ."

A few seconds passed, then she laughed, low and deep and husky.

"Breakfast can wait," she said.

She pushed him back on the bed and straddled his hips.

❖————❖

Forty-five minutes later, Jane roamed through the *Vicksburg Lady*'s main casino, doing a quick scan of the patrons' faces on the off chance that she'd come across Marybeth Traynor and her boyfriend Seth.

True, it was a day early for their anticipated arrival at the casino, but Jane was feeling . . . well, lucky. Blessed. As if she couldn't lose even if she tried. And it was all because of Nick.

She smiled and almost hugged herself with joy as the memories of their night together swamped her.

Okay, so he hadn't *exactly* told her that he loved her, but he had talked about a future together, so she knew that he cared for her—deeply too.

Since she was feeling so downright invincible at the moment, she figured checking out the casino for signs of her runaway would be worth a shot . . . especially since her breakfast had been postponed for another hour because of Nick's last-minute phone call from his father—problems with the family business, Nick had told her with an apologetic smile and a kiss on the cheek. He had suggested he meet her back at her motel at eleven-fifteen for brunch at the Benedict Inn. She'd agreed, then she'd decided to do a quick run through the casino on her way to her room to shower and change.

It was a good thing, too, Jane thought, coming

to a complete stop next to a row of slot machines. Her smile deepened into a grin.

Seth was nowhere to be seen, but Marybeth Traynor certainly was. She sat, big as life, next to one of the slots, smoking a cigarette and looking as miserably angst ridden as only an economically advantaged seventeen-year-old can.

Amazing, Jane thought, walking toward the girl. Every hand Jane played lately seemed to come up aces. It was as if she was on the kind of winning streak that her father used to dream about but never quite got.

"Hi," Jane said, planting herself squarely in front of Marybeth to prevent a sudden break for the nearest exit.

Marybeth jumped, then her pale blue eyes went as hard as flint. "Am I supposed to know you or something?"

"No, but I know you, Marybeth. My name is Jane Steele . . . I'm a private investigator."

Marybeth bit her bottom lip, suddenly looking far less brave than she had only moments before.

"Daddy sent you?"

"Uh-huh."

"Figures." She flicked ash toward the tray and missed. "Look, you're just wasting your time. You can't make me go back with you. I'm almost eighteen. I can do whatever I want, and Daddy can't stop me."

"That's just the thing," Jane said softly. "You're *almost* eighteen. Until your next birthday, state law says your daddy can make you go back home with him if he wants to, but I'm not here to drag you back to Jackson. He only hired me to find you, so he could talk to you."

"Daddy wants to talk?" Her voice cracked. "That'd be a first," she said, wrapping her arms across her chest. "All he ever used to do was yell."

Jane regarded the teenager for a moment. When Jane had taken the case, she had thought Marybeth was just another spoiled little rich girl rebelling against life. Now that Jane had actually met her . . .

"Your father told me what happened at the dance," Jane said slowly. "He lost his temper, and he said a lot of things that he's sorry about. But he loves you, Marybeth. He only wants what is best for you."

"Yeah, well, Seth is what's best for me," Marybeth said, taking another hit off her cigarette. "Why can't Daddy realize that?"

As though on cue, a tall, young man—sporting a scraggly goatee, long curly blond hair, a nose ring through his left nostril, and a definite scowl— walked toward them. He withdrew his right hand from the pocket of his oversize faded jeans and slid his arm protectively around Marybeth's shoulder.

"I don't know, Marybeth," Jane said. "Why don't you give your father a call and ask him yourself?"

"Yeah, right."

"Look," Jane said, "no matter how old you get,

he's always going to think of you as his little girl . . . just as you're always going to think of him as some superhero even though you know he has feet of clay. That's just the way these things work."

Her relationship with her own father had been no different, Jane acknowledged, at least with the superhero's feet of clay part. She had always known that his addiction to cards and the adrenaline rush of the game wasn't the fault of organized gambling. It was caused by his own inadequacies as a person. Even so, it made it easier for her to think of him as Superman felled by a deadly dose of kryptonite rather than as a man destroyed by a fatal character flaw.

It still did.

"Give him a break, Marybeth," Jane said. "Better yet, give yourself one."

Marybeth glanced up at Seth.

He nodded. "Call him," he said.

Marybeth sighed and stubbed out her cigarette in the overflowing ashtray.

"Okay, I'll call him," she said. "But I'm not promising any warm and fuzzy family reunions or anything."

"No promises expected," Jane said.

Although with Marybeth's tear-filled eyes—and with the worry and concern so evident in Daddy Traynor's voice the last time Jane spoke with him—the safe money would be on that reunion taking place before nightfall.

Jane smiled and wanted to hug herself again.

Now if only her lucky streak would hold a little longer until she got that one big win . . . the one where Tidwell and the *Lady* were put permanently out of business.

And she got to spend forever locked in Nick's arms.

He had to tell her.

Nick stood outside Jane's room at the Econo Lodge, with his hands shoved into his coat pockets, trying to ward off the chill of the morning when he knew his problem was more likely a chill of the soul.

¡Dios! he thought. He'd really screwed things up, possibly even past the point of reparation. But haranguing himself over what he should have done but didn't would not help matters now. He had to level with Jane about his being a Benedict, and he had to do it before things had a chance to get any worse.

Nick took a deep breath and rapped on the door. He heard a muffled response from inside, silence, then the sound of locks being turned over. The door popped open.

"Hi," Jane said, sounding breathless. "I'm sorry, but I'm running a little late."

She was wearing a bulky white terry cloth robe that struck her just about her knees, and her hair hung limp and damp around her shoulders as though she'd just gotten out of the shower.

He decided he'd never seen anything more

beautiful in his entire life. He swallowed hard and leaned down to kiss her cheek. She smelled of Jane, all lilacs and springtime. He wished that he could fill his lungs with the scent of her and keep it with him forever.

"I, ah, thought you'd have been pacing the room waiting for me," he said.

She shook her head and went back to the bathroom. "I just got here myself a little while ago."

"Oh?"

He slowly followed her. He tried to smile but his face hurt too damn much to quite make it.

"So where've you been?" he asked. "Wasn't the plan for you to come straight back here to take a shower and change for brunch?"

"Uh-huh," she said. "But I decided to take a quick run through the *Lady* first. I had a hunch that Marybeth Traynor—"

"That's your missing persons case, isn't it?"

"Right," she said, and smiled at him as though she were pleased that he'd remembered. "I thought she might have turned up here a day early."

"From the way you're floating on air right now, I take it that she did?"

"Right again."

She flipped the switch on her blow-dryer and tossed her damp hair over her head. Then, while shouting over the roar of the dryer, Jane filled him in on the details of her conversation with Marybeth and of the teenager's subsequent talk with her father.

"Daddy Traynor is currently en route to Vicksburg for a long overdue heart-to-heart with his daughter," Jane concluded, sliding the dryer onto the counter.

She reached for her brush and raked it through her hair. It shone under the florescent lights like mahogany-colored silk. He wanted to reach over and stroke her hair, wanted to feel it slide, warm and soft, through his fingers, but he fought the urge.

He knew that once he started touching her, he wouldn't be able to stop . . . and they had far too much to discuss for him to let his libido sidetrack him.

"Bill Traynor says he's extremely hopeful everything will work out between them," Jane added. "In fact, he's promised the agency a substantial bonus for services rendered."

"That's great," Nick murmured. "Congratulations." He leaned down and kissed her right temple. "I guess this calls for a celebration."

A slow smile slid across her face. Still holding the brush in her hand, she wound her arms around his waist and hugged him.

"So what kind of celebration did you have in mind?" she asked huskily. "Something public with lots of people around us . . . or something private with just the two of us?"

His heart started to pound. His body tightened. He slowly moved his palms along her arms to rest on her shoulders, feeling the soft terry cloth rustle beneath his fingers.

Don't, he told himself. He had to stay focused because he had to talk to her, about his family and hers. They had to discuss what he felt for her and what he suspected she felt for him. Then he had to make her understand. It wasn't as if he didn't sympathize with her feeling the way that she did about organized gambling. It was just that she was wrong to think that the entire industry was corrupt because of the bad hand her father had been dealt in life.

He glided his fingers along her jaw. *So, tell her*, he ordered himself. *Now*.

He took a deep breath. "Janie . . ."

"Yes?"

Her lips were parted slightly, and her eyes were so deeply green that he felt as if he'd lose his soul if he stared into them for too long.

"I . . ." He took another deep breath and gathered his courage. "Why can't we have both kinds of a celebration?" he asked, chickening out. "One public, another intensely private?"

Her smile deepened. "Maybe start with champagne brunch at the Benedict Inn . . . followed by more champagne up in your room . . . then spend the day making love?"

Memories assailed him: The taste of her skin . . . the silkiness of her heat when he slid into her body . . . the sheer breathlessness of her voice when she called out his name as she came.

He felt the muscles around his heart start to constrict. "It would work for me," he said huskily.

She gave him another hug, then released him. "It would work for me, too, *mi amor*, but we need to be practical right now. We've got Tidwell to deal with, and we have a thousand things to discuss."

"A thousand and one," he said softly.

But he seemed to be too much of a *cobarde*, a damned coward, to initiate the conversation on that thousand and first, even though he knew what he had to lose if they didn't talk before she found out who he really was from someone else.

"At least that," she agreed. Then she gave him a speculative glance out of the corner of her eye. "But finalizing our plans for the sting shouldn't take all day. I mean, everything is already set up. All that's really left to do is install the video camera in the game room."

He smiled. "And your pals, the former jewel thieves, will be here the day of the game to take care of that."

"Exactly."

She moved into his arms again. He let his hands slide around her waist, wishing he never had to let her go and vowing to himself that one day he wouldn't.

"So let's see," she went on. "We've already identified which games on board the *Lady* are rigged, and we know that they're all linked to the malfunctioning video recorder in the surveillance room. Coupled with the info the agency's resident computer whiz uncovered about Tidwell's employment history, we ought to have a strong case for arguing that he is the one behind everything, even if he doesn't decide to fleece you in the card game."

"Yeah, but my guess is Tidwell will try. He's spent the last week fattening me up for the kill, so why shouldn't he follow through? And if the gaming commission doesn't want to act on what we've uncovered, Benedict Casinos damn sure will."

In fact, when Nick had filled his father in on the latest developments a short time earlier, Sid Benedict had nearly gone ballistic. Particularly when he heard the part where Steele Angel's "resident computer whiz"—who was actually a sixteen-year-old hacker named Tyrone—had been able to learn with a few clicks of the computer keys that Tidwell had been dismissed from a New Jersey casino three years earlier under what could best be described as questionable circumstances.

Jane laughed and eased out of his arms. "I wouldn't bet too much money on Benedict Casinos doing anything about Tidwell if I were you."

He frowned. "What is that supposed to mean?"

She shrugged. "It means that I don't think they care one way or the other. If they did, they'd have stopped Tidwell long before now."

She brushed past him and headed for the other room.

"Maybe they didn't know what he was doing," he said, following her. "He's only been running the casino for what? Six weeks now?"

"That's no excuse and you know it." She opened the closet and rummaged through her clothes. "It's their casino, Nick. Their responsibility to keep everything honest. Hell, for all we know, Benedicts could be receiving a kickback from Tidwell for all the rigged games he's running on board the *Lady*."

Her words chilled him to the bone. "Is *that* what you think is going on here?" he asked.

She glanced back at him. "No, but it's a possibility we can't afford to overlook."

He regarded her for a long moment. "Maybe with other casinos," he said quietly, "but not with the Benedict Casinos."

Now it was her turn to give him a careful perusal. "Oh? And what makes you so sure?"

"Their reputation for one. They've operated casinos of one kind or another for over a century without a single hint of impropriety. They've always promised to run an honest house, and they always have."

"I've seen the plaque over the gangplank," she said, tossing him a grin.

She carried a blue-and-gray-striped sweater and a pair of blue jeans back into the bathroom and closed the door behind her.

"Only I wasn't all that impressed," she called out to him.

His frown deepened into a scowl.

"I know how you feel about casinos and about the people who run them," he said. "From what you've been through with your father, you're probably even partially justified in feeling that way. But you're wrong about the Benedicts. They don't rip off their customers. Hell, they don't even take advantage of them if they can help it."

"Oh, please!"

Her voice was muffled by the door, but her note of skepticism came through loud and clear.

"It's true," he told her. "For starters, if they suspected a patron was a compulsive gambler on a downward spiral, they'd ask him to leave the casino. And they also don't allow players to remain at the table if it's obvious that they're too drunk to know when to quit. Dealers, pit bosses, even the cocktail waitresses—they're all subject to immediate suspension if they don't pull the plug on a player who is out of control."

"You make them sound like a bunch of saints."

"Not saints. But not sinners, either. Just decent people providing an honest game of chance for those willing to take the risk. But then, that's the way Benedicts have done things ever since Nathaniel Benedict opened a gambling parlor in San Francisco during the gold rush days . . . and that's the way we'll *always* do things."

Silence. She said not a word, not even so much as a sound in response.

Then it hit him. Exactly what he'd said. *That's the way we'll always do things.*

We. Implying that he and the Benedict Casinos were one and the same.

Damn, he thought, cursing his own stupidity. This wasn't the way that he'd wanted to tell her, not by a long shot.

"*¿Cara?*" he asked softly.

She slowly opened the door. She'd changed into the sweater and jeans. With her long dark hair tumbling around her shoulders, she looked as breathtakingly beautiful as ever, but there was a coldness in her eyes that nearly ripped his heart to pieces.

"*We?*"

It was all she said.

Then again, it was all she needed to say.

He swallowed. "We," he said, softer now.

A few seconds ticked by, then he took a deep breath.

"I haven't been totally honest with you, Janie . . . about my name . . . about the reason I came to the *Vicksburg Lady* . . . about a lot of little things."

Jane continued to stare at him, feeling both numb and sick to her stomach and not sure which emotion was the stronger of the two.

"What . . . what are you saying?" she asked.

His gaze didn't waver. "That Valdez is my mother's maiden name . . . and the family business I said I no longer had any interest in is Benedict Casinos."

She felt her cheeks begin to flame, then the numbness set in for real. It spread through her veins like some kind of anesthetizing drug, deadening her emotions until she felt nothing at all.

"I . . . see," she murmured.

And in a crazy kind of way, she did.

After all, she'd never quite believed that Nick was a professional gambler—especially since he'd denied it at every opportunity—yet he'd deliberately set himself up as bait with Tidwell. What's more, Nick had always seemed to know so much about the business, both about sleight of hand card tricks and about the myriad ways one could rig every game in a casino.

"Like I told you," he went on, "I retired about ten days ago. I used to be the Chief Financial Officer . . . Corporate holdings are considerable, and except for a few idiosyncracies, the business is run like any other. Still, those idiosyncracies . . . well, let's just say I'd had enough."

He shoved his hands back into the pockets of his coat and looked down at the floor.

"I was ready to head for Mississippi to inspect the horse property when my father approached me. He'd received a letter from an elderly female customer who accused him of having a too tight slot machine on board the *Lady*. Dad takes those kind of accusations seriously. Although he really wasn't expecting for me to find any problems, he asked me to look into it while I was down here. I agreed, which is why I checked into the hotel as a high roller named Nick Valdez. During my first run through the casino, I stumbled across the rigged roulette wheel . . . and then the poker game where I saw you."

He looked up to meet her gaze. Pain shadowed his eyes. Regret too. She felt something stir inside her, but clamped down hard on the emotion.

"*Cara*, believe me," he said. "I never wanted to lie to you."

"Then why did you?"

He shrugged. "Fear. Stupidity. Take your pick. In the beginning, it was because I wasn't sure if I could trust you to keep my identity a secret. Later . . ." He sighed. "Later, you'd made it so clear how you felt about my family, about anyone who ran a casino, I was afraid to. But I did try last night in my room," he reminded her quietly. "Only you told me that nothing—not who I was or what I used to do for a living—would ever matter to you."

She just stared at him. "We both said a lot of things last night."

"Yeah, but I meant all of mine."

She didn't answer him. She didn't know how.

"Look." He raked his fingers through his hair as though he was growing frustrated. "My being a Benedict, it's just a detail, *cara*. It doesn't change who I really am . . . It doesn't change how I feel about you . . . and it shouldn't change how you feel about me."

"You're right," she said in a voice just as calm and logical as his had been. "It shouldn't."

He stared at her. "But it does, right?"

Now it was her turn to shrug.

He muttered a curse under his breath and looked away.

"Don't," she told him. "We agreed on one night of passion . . . one night to go completely *loco de amor* with each other's body so we could get this—whatever it is we feel for each other—out of our collective systems. I promised you there'd be no regrets, and there won't be. Not even now. But . . ."

He glanced back at her.

She took a deep breath. "But our night together is over. It's time for the fantasy to end and for us to get back to reality."

"But you're not out of my system," he said. "Not by a long damn shot."

He grasped her arm. The heat of his fingertips seared through her skin to brand her soul with his touch. She shuddered.

"And I don't think that I'm out of yours," he added huskily.

He wasn't, she silently acknowledged. But then, something told her that he'd never truly be, either. Still . . .

She took a deep breath. "I . . . I'm sorry."

His gaze searched hers for a moment, then he released her arm.

"So am I," he whispered. "For us both."

The next couple of hours were some of the worst in Nick's memory. They had their brunch at the Benedict Inn just as they'd planned, but he doubted if either one of them tasted much of the food. He had lost his appetite around the time that he'd finally leveled with Jane about who he was and her eyes had turned cold and unforgiving. Instead of eating, Nick merely went through the motions and pushed his eggs around his plate as they discussed the final details for their sting. But he watched Jane every chance he got, willing her to say something, anything that would give him hope that she still cared.

She didn't say a word.

For that matter, she didn't even look directly at him if she could help it. He could have been a stranger for all the emotion she seemed to invest in him, and it hurt. It hurt a lot. If she'd shown anger, if she'd screamed at him in outrage at his duplicity, he could have dealt with it. He could have dealt with almost anything but the indifference, because the indifference made him think that she didn't care about him at all, which was what scared him the most.

So Nick said nothing in return about what he felt for her . . . even though he loved her . . . even though he felt so tied up in her soul that he didn't know where he left off and where she began. He said nothing.

And the silence between them grew until it almost became deafening.

NINE

At a few minutes past one on the day of the poker game, Jane sat in Miss Penny's Diner and slowly stirred artificial sweetener into her cup of coffee. She was only half listening as Remy Ballou—who was already dressed in the casino maintenance uniform that he'd be wearing when he went on board the *Lady*—explained their plan for recording the game.

Jane was only half listening because she was sitting next to Nick in one of the coffee shop's red-vinyl-covered booths. Their bodies didn't touch—in fact, they sat as far apart from each other as the booth would allow, with their folded coats acting as a barrier—but they were close enough for his undeniable masculinity to overwhelm her senses and affect her concentration, although she did her best to pretend otherwise, just as she had been doing ever since their fight in her motel room. Try as she might, though, she couldn't ignore him. Not for the past two days and certainly not now. Nor could she ignore the yearnings of her heart, although she knew that she could never allow herself to give in to them.

She'd already made a fool out of herself over the man once. She had no intention of doing it a second time.

"Basically," Remy said in his low Cajun drawl, "we're just going to redirect the video feed from the casino's own surveillance camera into our recorder, which we'll store in Jane's locker back in the employee lounge."

Nick nodded, but didn't look convinced. "How long will the rewiring take?"

"Five minutes, tops," Remy said. "And it'll be more like clamping onto the existing wiring than rerunning any cables. All we're planning to do is have the camera reroute its signal to our remote, rather than to the surveillance room. The receiver is small but it's powerful. There shouldn't be any problems in picking up the feed."

Michael Ann O'Donnell Ballou nodded and reached for another french fry off her husband's plate. She was four months pregnant with twin boys, and was eating enough to feed a small army. She had finished off her own chef salad and then started in on Remy's fries, not that he seemed to mind. They had held hands all during lunch, and Remy looked at Mike with such unabashed adoration that Jane envied her friend's happiness. Especially since Jane was feeling sorry for herself just then.

"We've used them before," Mike said. "Dozens of times. The chance for a screwup is minimal. Of course, if you prefer, we could also have you wear a hidden camera. We have one that looks just like a tie clasp. Its range is limited, but it should be able to feed into the employee lounge without any problems."

"But you don't recommend it?" Nick asked.

Mike shrugged. "Rerouting the surveillance camera feed will give you a better shot of the action because the camera is installed above the table. If you're wearing a lapel camera, your POV will be limited."

"I agree," Remy said. "Rerouting the security feed is your best bet."

"Then let's do it," Nick murmured, tossing his crumpled napkin onto the table.

Remy nodded. "Fine. I've got my equipment out in the car. You can keep an eye out for security while I modify the video feed."

"Deal."

"Just be careful," Jane murmured, reaching for Nick's coat. "Barbara Weems likes to make a midday sweep through the casino, and Tidwell often accompanies her."

"No problem," Nick said.

She handed him his coat. His fingers accidentally slid over hers as he took the coat from her. It was like getting a jolt of pure electricity shot straight through to her core. Their gazes locked. For a moment, she thought she saw a flicker of something cross his face—need, hunger, sorrow. Maybe a combination of all three. For a moment, she thought he was going to say something to her—like how he was sorry that they had argued or that he loved her more than he did life. But the moment passed.

Nick looked away, then removed his hand from hers and slid out of the booth. She felt a part of her soul start to shrivel and die.

"We'll be careful," Remy promised. He leaned over and gave Mike a kiss on her cheek. "And we'll be back before you can miss us."

Seconds later, Nick and Remy were gone. Jane slumped back in the booth with a heavy sigh and took a long swallow of coffee.

"It'll be okay," Mike said quietly. "Remy's an old hand at conning his way into all kinds of places. He knows what he's doing."

"I know."

Jane glanced out the window and watched Nick and Remy make their way through the parking lot. Her gaze lingered on Nick, on the way he moved and how the wind whipped through his dark hair.

Mike smiled. "Nick can take care of himself, too, if that's what is worrying you." Then Mike gave Jane a curious once-over. "Speaking of which, what's up with you and him, anyway?"

Jane felt herself start to blush. "I . . . nothing," she said.

"Oh, I'd say it was definitely something. I've never seen two people spend so much time trying to pretend that they're not aware of the other than you two do."

Jane took a sip of coffee. "Is it that obvious?"

"Afraid so."

Jane shrugged. "We had a thing," she said. "It's over now . . . It's for the best, anyway. The Traynor case is closed and the card game is scheduled for this evening, so there's no reason for me to stay in Vicksburg. Besides, Nick . . ."

"Is a Benedict?" Mike supplied with a smile. "Didn't anyone ever tell you that it's not fair to hold a man's entire family tree against him? And from what I hear, the Benedicts are considered one of the good guys in the business."

Jane frowned. "It . . . you don't understand."

Mike was quiet for a moment. "No, I think *you're* the one who doesn't understand, Jane. The man is in love with you."

"Yeah, well," Jane muttered under her breath, and took another sip of coffee. "I'm in love with him too. But what possible difference does any of *that* make in the major scheme of things?"

"A lot actually." Mike reached for her water glass.

Jane glanced up.

"When you get right down to it," Mike went on, "it's the only thing that does matter. Loving someone . . . having them love you back. As long as you have that, you can overcome anything."

"Maybe," Jane said.

"Always," Mike said, and slid her hand across her stomach. She radiated contentment. "Whatever he's done, whatever has happened between you, it's not as important as what you still feel for each other. Take it from someone who's been there."

Jane let her gaze slip toward the window again. She could barely make out the top of Nick's head as he and Remy, who was now carrying a large silver metal case in one hand, disappeared up the gangplank toward the casino.

"Maybe," Jane whispered again, wishing that she had the courage to risk her heart one more time, but knowing she was probably too afraid to try.

Nick clamped his cigar between his teeth and watched Tidwell deal the third, and probably last, hand of the poker game. Nick thought it would be the last hand because the casino manager had just switched to a fresh deck, and this one had the same subtle markings as the deck used in Pearce's game the week before. What's more, Tidwell was beginning to deal off the bottom, which Nick felt could only mean that the casino manager was moving in for the kill.

Nick glanced at Jane, who was pretending to check her hair in the gilded mirror at the wet bar across the room. Their gazes met in the mirror's reflection. She gave him a slight nod to show that she'd seen both Tidwell's new deck and the way he was dealing them. Then she raised her eyes in the direction of the security camera, reminding Nick that, more importantly, the camera would have seen everything, too, and recorded it all for posterity.

Nick smiled and turned over his cards. The suits were a surprise, but everything else was what their markings had suggested they'd be: A pair of eights, a jack, a ten, and a three.

They'd been playing for the better part of an hour, and Tidwell seemed to be following the same plan the dealer had used in Pearce's game—namely, the first couple of hands had proceeded without incident, and the pot had grown progressively larger. By Nick's calculations, it now totaled close to thirty thousand dollars and showed no signs of tapering off.

There were four other players at the table, mostly local businessmen who enjoyed high stakes poker according to Tidwell's introductions. None of them appeared to be aware that Tidwell had invited them to a crooked game, though, nor that he had switched to a marked deck.

Nick sorted his cards and took a puff off his cigar. Jane started to walk back to the table, carrying two tall glasses of club soda in her hands. He let his gaze slide over her again as he set his cigar in the ashtray. She was wearing a tight, formfitting black dress, and she'd pulled her hair up in an elegant twist. She looked so beautiful, he felt his heart begin to ache.

The tension between them was still there, but it was showing signs of breaking. Then again, maybe he was the one who was breaking from the strain. He'd wanted to give her time to think things through and had hoped that she would eventually come around to realizing that they belonged together . . . and that they could make every dream in their hearts become reality if they tried.

He still felt that way, although he was becoming increasingly aware that time was a commodity which they both had in limited quantities . . . although what he was going to do to fix things between them, and when, he wasn't quite sure.

"Mr. Reardon?" Tidwell murmured, nodding toward a silver-haired man in his late sixties. "Your opening bid, please?"

"One thousand," the man said, and tossed in a chip.

The man on Reardon's immediate left chuckled and added two more. "Why don't we make it two?"

"Mr. Benning?" Tidwell murmured, nodding at the overweight, balding man next in line.

"Two's fine with me."

Two more poker chips hit the kitty.

Jane leaned down and gave Nick his drink. The scent of her perfume wafted over him. It was as soft as a caress, and he responded to it with both his body and his soul.

"Tidwell's holding four aces," she whispered against his ear.

He turned his head slightly to meet her gaze. "Thanks."

She regarded him for a moment, not with the coldness or the indifference she'd shown over the past two days, but with a tenderness that warmed him throughout. Then she brushed her lips lightly over his. He knew the kiss was supposed to be for Tidwell's benefit. Still, it was sweet and soft and seeped in the promise of so much heat that it made Nick's heart begin to sing for the first time in days.

"My pleasure, *mi amor*," she whispered back.

"*Tu eres mi único placer, mi amor*," he murmured without thinking, because his only pleasure was her and always would be.

Jane smiled and stroked her hand across his face, then moved over to her chair next to the wall, although the warmth of her fingertips lingered with him long after.

"Mr. Valdez?" Tidwell asked.

Unable to mask a grin, Nick turned back to the table and reached for his pile of chips. Suddenly, the game couldn't be over fast enough to suit him.

"I'm feeling luckier than usual tonight, *amigos*," he said. "Let's make it five, shall we?"

A grin slid across Tidwell's face as well. "The game has no cap, Mr. Valdez. Five it is."

"Son of a bitch!"

Reardon slammed his fist down on the table in disgust as his three queens were beaten by Tidwell's four aces some fifteen minutes later. The other locals just shrugged and reached for their respective jackets. The game was officially over.

Jane slowly stood. She had lost track of the betting during the game, but she suspected the final pot was somewhere near fifty grand. Since fifteen thousand of that was Reardon's own contribution to Tidwell's personal retirement fund, she could well understand Reardon's annoyance at having lost.

"Sorry, Mr. Reardon," Tidwell said, raking the pile of chips toward him.

Once again, the image of a lion sprang into Jane's head, only this one had just gorged himself on his prey and was now ready to lick his chops and bask in the sun for a while.

"Better luck next time, huh?"

"Next time, hell," Reardon grumbled. "My luck seems to be nothing but bad ever since I started coming to this place."

Reardon reached for his half-drunk glass of bourbon and water and finished it off in one swig.

Nick stubbed out his cigar in the heavy crystal ashtray. His hand slid across three of his discarded cards, each subtly marked like the rest, and palmed them as he rose to his feet.

"Then you're past due for a change of fortunes, my friend," Nick murmured. He slid the hand containing the marked cards into his jacket pocket. "Every losing streak has to end sometime, just as does every lucky streak . . . even the one enjoyed by our host."

Tidwell started to tuck the cards into a long plastic tray, apparently unaware that some were missing. "It's called a game of chance, gentlemen, because you take a chance when you sit down to play. I'm sorry the game didn't turn out the way you'd both hoped it would."

Nick flashed both dimples at Tidwell. "Oh, I wouldn't say that. I for one have no complaints over the way the evening has gone." Nick extended his hand to Jane. "In fact, I couldn't be happier about certain aspects of it," he added.

She was at his side in an instant. He gave her a kiss on her cheek, then they started toward the door without a backward glance.

She tilted her head toward his when they reached the hallway. "Now what?" she whispered.

"First we get the tape," he murmured, speaking low enough so only she could hear. "We make sure Remy's receiver did the trick, then we make a few calls and confront Tidwell with what we have."

"Sounds good to me. Then we can finally pop the cork on the champagne bottle and celebrate Tidwell's downfall."

Nick slid his hand around her waist. His fingertips scorched through the fabric of her dress and made her shiver. It felt so good to have him touch her, so good to feel him next to her.

"All in due time, *cara*," he agreed.

There was a huskiness and a hunger in his voice that intensified her shivers a hundredfold. He glanced down at her and smiled. "First, though, we need to talk . . . about you and me and where we go from here."

She smiled and hugged him back. She couldn't have expressed it better herself.

An hour later, Nick held Jane's hand as they walked down the hallway toward Tidwell's private office. They were the first of a small parade consisting of the two casino security officers, a couple of Warren County Sheriff's deputies, an assistant D.A. with a stack full of hastily prepared legal documents, and an extremely annoyed representative from the state gaming commission named Branson Jones.

Jones was annoyed because he'd been pulled away from his second wedding anniversary celebration to handle Tidwell. As a result, the harried bureaucrat had promised to invent a few broken ordinances to charge Tidwell with if the current crop didn't hold.

But Nick suspected the charges would all stick. Remy's receiver had done everything he and Mike had claimed it would, and Tidwell's bottom-of-the-deck dealing toward the end of the game had been impossible to miss on tape. Coupled with the marked cards Nick had taken from the game room, and the mountain of other circumstantial evidence that he and Jane had been able to amass over the past week, Nick had felt confident enough to phone the authorities, who had moved with amazing speed. Now, all that was left to do was confront Tidwell.

Nick slowed as they rounded the corner. Angry voices—one male, the other female—ricocheted down the hallway from the direction of Tidwell's office.

Nick stopped in front of the door and glanced at Jane. She shrugged.

". . . worthless bastard!" shouted Barbara Weems from inside the office. "You've done nothing but use me from the beginning, haven't you?"

"Calm down," Tidwell yelled back. "You don't know what you're talking about."

"The hell I don't! I may have been walking around here in a fog for six weeks now, but the fog has lifted, and I don't like what I see, Bob. I don't like it one bit."

"Barbara . . ."

"You've been rigging the games on board the *Lady*," she went on. "And you've been using me to cover your ass. That's why you gave me the job as acting security chief, wasn't it? So you could rip off everybody with no one the wiser?"

"No. Of course not. Sweetheart, let's sit down and talk this over like sensible adults."

"Jerk," Jane mumbled under her breath.

Nick squeezed her hand. The descriptive noun he had in mind for Tidwell was considerably more colorful.

"Half of my staff thinks I'm stupid," Barbara said. "The other half thinks I'm scum. I can't say I blame them for thinking either, because it's obvious I can't handle the job as security chief. But before I quit, I'm calling Benedict Casinos' corporate offices and telling them exactly what you're up to down here."

"That . . . would be very stupid." Tidwell's voice had turned cold and deadly.

Nick didn't bother to wait for the rest of Tidwell's response. Nick grasped the doorknob and gave it a turn.

Barbara stood at Tidwell's desk with her arms folded against her chest. She glanced over her shoulder at the door. Her eyes were red and bloodshot, as though she were close to tears.

Tidwell looked more disconcerted than tearful. He was flushed, and his sandy blond hair uncharacteristically unkempt. He smoothed it back and attempted to compose himself.

"Mr. Valdez," he murmured, rebuttoning his jacket. "I'm sorry, but this . . . this isn't a good time to talk."

"I can imagine," Nick said dryly, walking into the room, still holding on to Jane's hand. "And you're right, Barbara. Tidwell has been using you to rip off the casino and its customers. But there's no need to call Benedict Casinos' corporate office to report him."

The other members of the parade walked through the door and spread out across the room. Tidwell's eyes began to bulge.

"You see, corporate already knows," Nick went on. "They know because I've told them."

Tidwell shook his head. "Mr. Valdez . . ."

"The name's not Valdez . . . it's Benedict. And as of right now, you're no longer employed by *Benedict's Vicksburg Lady* . . . but that's the least of your problems, I assure you."

The sheriff's deputies and the assistant D.A. moved into position. The D.A. handed one of the deputies a legal document.

"Robert James Tidwell," the deputy with the paper said while the second one pulled out a pair of handcuffs. "We have a warrant for your arrest." Then the deputy listed the charges filed against Tidwell and began to read the casino manager his rights.

"Whoa," Tidwell said, backing up. "Wait a minute. I think there's been some kind of mistake here."

"Damn right there has," Branson Jones mumbled, stepping into the fray. "And you made it, mister. By the time I'm through with you, you won't even be able to get a *dog* license in this state without the governor's handwritten okay . . . and I wouldn't hold my breath on getting it even then."

Barbara Weems started to laugh. "I hope you rot," she said bitterly, then walked toward the bar. She opened the cabinet doors and quietly began to pour herself a drink.

The next half hour was a blur of activity. Tidwell's bravado deserted him around the time the deputies slapped on the handcuffs, but he didn't break down and confess. Instead, he demanded to see an attorney, which the deputies assured him would be provided once they reached the station, then they escorted him out the door.

After finishing her drink and pouring another, Barbara Weems calmly advised that she had shut down all the games hooked up to the malfunctioning video recorder before confronting Tidwell. She provided the names of the five dealers and security personnel she suspected were involved in pulling off Tidwell's scam, then she officially tendered her resignation and left the room.

Those casino employees that she'd named who were still on board the *Lady* were quickly rounded up by security, including the dealer from Pearce's poker game. He admitted he'd been running crooked games at the urging of Tidwell and agreed to testify to Tidwell's orchestration of the scam at trial. The assistant D.A. promised to have warrants issued for the remaining suspects by daybreak, then called it a night.

That left Branson Jones, who looked far less annoyed than when he'd gotten there. He explained, almost apologetically, that a detailed investigation of the casino would be undertaken the next morning. However, he saw no reason to close the *Lady* down since Benedict Casinos had taken steps to correct the problem with Tidwell. Then he left as well, advising that he wanted to enjoy whatever remained of his wedding anniversary celebration with his wife and infant daughter.

Nick turned to Jane as soon as the door closed and they were alone.

She gave him a smile. "Well," she said, and slid the silver metal straps of her evening bag onto her shoulder. "Tidwell's off to jail, probably for a very long time, and the rigged games are finally closed down . . . I guess we accomplished everything that we set out to in our partnership."

He smiled back at her. "Oh, not quite everything, *cara.*"

He slipped his hands around her waist and gave her a kiss whose passion began somewhere in his soul.

Jane's heart began to pound as the kiss deepened and grew. She felt herself start to flush, then the flush turned into a fire. Its heat began in her toes, and it worked its way up her body until she felt as though she'd burst into flames at any second.

"I've missed you so much," he murmured huskily. "These past two days have been absolute hell . . . having to see you but not being able to touch you . . . wanting to talk to you but being too afraid of what you'd say to me to take the chance."

"I know," she said. "I'm sorry."

"Me too. For everything. I should have leveled with you in the beginning about my being a Benedict—"

"But you couldn't take that risk," she interrupted him. "Besides, you were right. Your being a Benedict, it's just a detail . . . It doesn't change who you are . . . or what we feel for each other."

He stroked her face. "Do you mean that?" he asked softly.

She nodded. "And I also realize that I've been wrong to blame my father's problems with cards on organized gambling. The truth is, he loved taking risks. If it hadn't been poker, he'd have found another vice."

He gave her a soft smile, then he kissed her again, more tenderly this time.

"So," he murmured, pulling back to look at her. "Does this mean we're okay?"

"It means we're better than okay," she told him.

She ran her hands under his jacket to encircle his waist and hugged him.

"You're sure?" he asked.

"Positive." She moved closer to him and grinned. "In fact, why don't we go back to your room, where I could show you just how okay everything is between us?"

He laughed and glided his hands down her back. "I'd like that," he said. "I'd like to spend the night making love with you . . . *¡Dios!* I'd like to spend the next week making love to you."

"The next week might be something of a problem, *mi amor*. I have to go back to Jackson tomorrow morning. Steele Angel needs me . . . and you've probably got dozens of things to take care of here at the casino."

He sighed. "You're right. Once the media hears about Tidwell, this place will likely turn into a three-ring circus. Every person who ever lost a dime in the casino will be coming back, demanding a refund. It'll be a P.R. disaster, but the *Lady* will survive it."

He pulled her closer until her breasts were crushed against his chest. The musk-laden scent of his cologne swamped her senses.

"I just want to make sure that *we* survive it," he said huskily. "I don't want to lose you, Janie."

"You won't," she told him.

His gaze searched hers for a long moment, then he sighed. "I wish I could be sure of that. You see, my schedule is going to be a little crazy for the next few months. First with the casino, then with buying the horse ranch. I'll probably be lousy company."

She smiled. "I won't mind."

"Yeah, but I will. You deserve better than that. You deserve better than me."

"Nick . . ."

He muttered a curse under his breath and released her. "If my divorce taught me anything, it's that I can't juggle a relationship with business. That's why I told myself that I wouldn't get involved with someone until I've gotten the ranch fully operational. *¡Dios, cara!* I don't want to hurt you. I don't think I could bear it."

A chill settled around her heart as she realized what he was trying to tell her. "It . . . it's okay," she said. "I'm not expecting more from you than you can give me. If all we can have together is one more night, then I can accept it."

He frowned. "But that's not what I'm saying at all. Janie, *mi amor*, I need more than one more night with you. I need all your nights and all your days. I need forever. It's just that—"

"It's okay," she said again. "We won't make promises, so we won't have regrets. Tomorrow, we'll head back to reality—me to Jackson, you to your responsibilities here—but for tonight . . . well, for tonight, we've still got our fantasy."

Since something told her that a fantasy would be all they could ever have together, she wrapped her arms around his neck and held him tight.

TEN

Nick jerked awake at a quarter to nine the next morning. He knew Jane was gone before he ever opened his eyes. He could feel her absence in the way the bed had grown cold and empty, much like his heart was quickly becoming.

"*¿Cara?*" he murmured, hoping against hope that he was wrong, hoping that she was only in the bathroom or perhaps curled up in one of the chairs, reading a magazine, not wanting to wake him.

But there was no answer.

Seconds passed, but he still wasn't willing to accept the truth that she'd slipped out of bed and left while he lay sleeping.

Nick opened his eyes and looked around the room. "Janie?" he called, louder this time.

Then he noticed that her coat, which had been flung across the chair next to the window, was no longer there. Neither was her purse, or her shoes, or her clothes, which had tumbled to a crumpled heap next to his on the floor as soon as they'd entered the room and fallen into each other's arms, kissing and touching and loving as though they'd been gripped by the same insatiable hunger.

"I'm not expecting more from you than you can give me," she'd said.

Her words came back to taunt him with a harshness that wounded the soul. As did what she'd said to him next.

"We won't make promises, so we won't have regrets. Tomorrow, we'll head back to reality—me to Jackson, you to your responsibilities here—but for tonight . . . well, for tonight, we've still got our fantasy."

He muttered a curse and threw off the covers.

Dios, but he'd been acting like a fool. True, they both had responsibilities, they both had obligations that they couldn't ignore, so he well understood why she'd had to return to Jackson. Hell, he even understood why she hadn't awakened him before she'd left—saying good-bye would have been too painful. What he didn't understand was why he'd let things get to this point in the first place. He should have insisted that they not ignore their hearts. He should have insisted that she stay with him, no matter what.

Most of all, though, he should have told her that he loved her.

Because now Jane was gone . . . and he wasn't all that confident she'd ever come back.

He reached for his pants and started to get

dressed, wondering if he still had time to catch her before she checked out of her motel. The phone began to ring.

He made a grab for the receiver, praying that it was her. "Janie?"

"Ah . . . Mr. Benedict?" The voice was male and vaguely familiar. "This is Aaron Fitzpatrick . . . from over in casino security? I don't mean to disturb you, but we've got several news crews camped out on the gangplank, waiting for a statement from somebody about Mr. Tidwell. Plus, there's a gentleman from the gaming commission who says you're expecting him. How do you want us to handle it?"

Nick raked a hand through his hair. The *Lady*. Tidwell. The fallout from the sting and the former casino manager's arrest. For a moment, Nick had almost forgotten it all.

"Just sit tight," he murmured. "I'll be there in five minutes." Which meant, unfortunately, that his talk with Jane would have to wait.

Nick sighed. He only hoped that they'd still have something to talk about when he was finished.

Five days later, Jane sat in her office at Steele Angel Investigations, feeling as though she were bogged down in a morass of paperwork. Since keeping busy left her with little time to think about Nick, she continued to push herself with twelve-hour workdays, much to her partners' frequently voiced disapproval.

Only the long hours didn't seem to help. She couldn't stop thinking about Nick, just as she couldn't get the taste of his mouth, or the heat of his skin, or the sound of his voice out of her head. What made it worse was that Tidwell's arrest was the current story of the hour. Each time she turned on the evening news, or picked up a newspaper, she'd find Nick's face plastered across it, and the all-consuming need for him would swamp over her again . . . even though she knew it was a need that she could never satisfy again.

Jane sighed and reached for her closing report on the Traynor case. A tap sounded on her door.

"Come in."

She glanced up and watched her two partners saunter into her office. Both, she decided, looked suspiciously smug about something, which sent her internal alarms into full alert.

"We've got a new client waiting for you in the conference room," Johnny said matter-of-factly.

Like all the other males in the Angel family, Johnny was a solid six feet of irresistible Southern charm and masculine good looks who could talk other people into—and himself out of—almost any situation imaginable. From the grin he was giving her, Jane began to wonder what particular kind of mischief he had planned for her.

"Yeah, and he's asking specifically for you," Kat piped in. She hopped on the edge of the desk and crossed her legs. She was wearing a red miniskirt and a white midriff sweater that set off her short auburn hair to stylish perfection.

"Why don't one of you guys handle it," Jane suggested. "I've got to finish these file reviews."

"No can do, sis," Kat said. "He says you're the only one who can help him . . . pity too 'cause he's a real honey."

Jane frowned. "He's insisting on seeing me? What's the case?"

"Missing person," Johnny said, taking a seat on the other side of the desk.

"It's so sad," Kat added. "He says the woman he loves has left him, and he needs Steele Angel's help to find her . . . although if you ask me, any woman would have to be crazy to leave a man like him."

"I don't know about crazy," Johnny said. "Just plain stubborn is probably more accurate."

Jane frowned. "So he has a wayward wife. Why drag me into it when Johnny's the pro at handling domestic dispute cases?"

Kat shook her head. "She's not his wife. Although I think he's planning to ask her as soon as he sees her again. You got that impression, didn't you?" she asked, turning to Johnny.

He grinned. "Yeah, I'd have to say that I did."

Jane glanced from Kat over to Johnny, and then back again. The look on their faces went way beyond smug, Jane decided. The wail of her internal alarm grew louder.

"Okay," she murmured. "So it's his girlfriend and not his wife. It's still a domestic dispute, which Johnny is better at handling than I am."

"But you're the one the client wants to have handle it," Kat said. She slid off the desk and grabbed Jane's hand, then started to drag her toward the door.

Johnny hopped off the desk and followed. "What's more, you're the *only* one who can solve this particular case," he added.

He opened the door and took Jane's elbow, then guided her through the reception area and over to the conference room.

Jane shook her head. "But—"

"No but's," Kat and Johnny said in unison.

Then before Jane could muster another protest, Johnny opened the door to the conference room, and Kat pushed Jane inside. Jane stumbled to a stop next to the table in the center of the room. Her gaze shot toward the window, where a tall, black-haired man stood, with his back to the door and his hands shoved into the pockets of his gray overcoat. She recognized him in a heartbeat.

"Nick?" she whispered, feeling suddenly confused.

He turned. He looked tired, she realized with a pang of concern. It was an emotional exhaustion, though, not a physical one, since the weariness seemed to radiate from his core. More than that, it was the kind of soul-depleting fatigue that comes from spending far too much time agonizing over wanting something you'd already told yourself that you can't have.

Knowing he looked as miserable as she'd been feeling herself made her heart begin to ache.

It ached for him.

And for her.

And for what they'd almost had but lost.

She heard the door close behind her but didn't move.

"Thanks for seeing me without an appointment, Ms. Steele," Nick said.

His voice no longer had the aura of playful sexiness that she'd always found so appealing. Instead, it was coated with a veneer of aloofness and professionalism, as though they were two strangers about to discuss a business transaction.

"My name is Nick Benedict," he said. "I assume your partners filled you in on my case?"

She stared at him for a long moment before answering. "They told me that you wanted to hire me to track down a missing girlfriend." She frowned at him. "Look, if this is your idea of a joke, I'm sorry but I don't find it at all funny."

She turned toward the door.

"It's no joke, Ms. Steele," he said. "You see, I'm afraid that I've lost the love of someone who means the world to me."

She stopped but didn't turn around.

"I don't know how to get her back," he went on. "I came here because I want to hire Steele Angel . . . I want to hire you . . . to help me accomplish two things that might, hopefully, bring her around."

Her heart simply stopped. She slowly turned. "And those two things are?" she asked.

His gaze locked with hers. "First, is to help me find her," he said. "She slipped out of my bed and out of my life five days ago without so much as a word of good-bye. I'm not sure, but I think she may have returned to her home here in Jackson."

Jane felt herself begin to flush. "And the second?"

"The second is to help me convince her what a fool I've been . . . about us, about so many things . . . and to ask her to come back to me. To stay with me this time. Forever."

"I see."

Jane folded her arms against her chest and glanced down at the carpeting.

"Are you sure that you really want her to come back?" she asked softly. "Forever can be an awfully long time, Mr. Benedict."

"Especially if you have to spend it alone," he said, his voice just as soft. "And, yes, I want her to come back. I'm only half alive without her . . . and I'm hoping she's missing me almost as much."

She was. So much so that it was practically killing her.

She slowly raised her head to look at him. "So why did she leave you, if you don't mind my asking?"

His gaze locked with hers. "I'm afraid you'll

have to ask her that yourself. My guess—and it's only a guess—is that it was because she felt I'd given her no choice. She probably thinks that I don't have room in my life to make a commitment. You see, the family business is undergoing something of a crisis right now. I'm technically retired but it's family, so I'm involved. And I'm buying a piece of horse property outside of Jackson. It's been a dream of mine for some time now, and dreams take a lot of hard work to turn them into reality."

"Both of which leave little time for long-term commitments."

He shrugged. "I never used to have much luck mixing business with romance, and I told her that. What I apparently forgot to tell her was that I thought things would be different this time, because what we had together was so special." His gaze searched hers. "I guess I assumed that she must know how I felt about her, when I should have told her."

Her heart began to pound. Her stomach did a somersault. She took a deep breath.

"You're right," she said. "Assuming things can be dangerous."

Then she paused a moment. "So how do you feel about her? Specifically, I mean?"

His gaze didn't waver. "I love her," he said. The huskiness and the heat had returned to his voice. "I want to spend the rest of my life making love to her, creating fantasies that we can both share . . . I want her to be my wife and the mother of my babies . . . I want her to be a part of my dreams, just as I want to be a part of hers. Is that . . . *specific enough* . . . for you, Ms. Steele, or should I go on?"

Happiness and joy welled up inside her like a geyser about to explode. She started to smile.

"Oh, it'll do for starters, I guess," she murmured.

He smiled back. "So what do you think?" he asked, skirting the table to move toward her. "Will you take my case? Or do you think that my chances of succeeding are too minuscule to warrant the effort?"

He stopped in front of her.

"I'll take your case, Mr. Benedict," she said. "I'll even waive my usual fee."

She slid her hands up his chest to rest on his shoulders. The warmth of his body seeped into her palms to drive the chill from her heart. For good, this time, she hoped.

"As for what I think of your chances," she went on. "They're excellent. In fact, I can guarantee a happy ending for you both."

"How so?" His hands moved to her waist. The heat of his fingertips made her shudder.

"Luckily for you, I moonlight as a *bruja*," she said huskily.

"Ahh," he murmured. "So you're one of those dark-haired enchantresses . . . My mother's people have warned me about your kind. You like to steal men's souls, don't you?"

She smiled. "Sometimes. Mostly, though, we just look into them to see what's really there."

He met her gaze, held it. "And what do you see when you look into my soul, *querida*?"

"The missing half of my own," she whispered.

She leaned up and kissed him, gently brushing her lips over his, wanting to savor the taste of his mouth against hers forever. She felt him sigh, then his hands moved down to grasp her buttocks, and he pulled her closer to him.

Nick decided that he didn't want to let her go. He wanted to hold her against him until the seasons changed and the years passed, until they'd grown old together and their babies were having babies of their own. But the need to breathe finally took hold of him, so he pulled away to gaze down at her in wonder.

Her face was flushed, and her eyes shown with love. It fed his heart until his soul rejoiced.

"I meant it," he said hoarsely, tracing the pad of his thumb over her mouth. "I love you, *cara*. I want to marry you."

"I love you too," she said, and he believed her with every fiber of his being.

"So will you marry me?" he asked.

He held his breath and waited for her answer.

The joy in her face said it all. "Absolutely." She breathed the word against his chin, then she slid her lips over his again.

He felt the damp warmth of her tongue pressing against his mouth, and he opened for her. Her tongue found his, and they started to move together, caressing, massaging, dancing the erotic tango that was theirs alone.

Time passed, and they continued to share slow, deep kisses that were unlike any he'd ever shared before, because he was kissing Jane and she loved him.

"Janie, *mi amor*," he said huskily. "Swear to me on my heart that you'll never leave me again. Because when I woke up and discovered that you were gone . . ."

He tightened his hold on her, unable to complete the sentence.

"I thought it would be better for us both if I just left," she murmured. "I didn't think you were ready for a commitment, and I knew I couldn't stand having anything less with you."

"But my soul made a commitment to you the first time you touched me," he said. "It just took my head a little longer to figure it out, that's all."

She hugged him until the scent of lilacs and springtime filled his lungs, and the last of his doubts about them and their future slipped away.

"Things are still going to be a little complicated for a while," he said. "My younger brother Antonio is coming out to take over the casino, but I'm still going to be needed on an advisory basis . . . but I promise you that my days working for the casino are over."

"It's okay," she said. "It's family. I understand. And I also understand that getting the ranch off the ground will take a lot of your time . . . just as running Steele Angel is going to take a lot of mine. Don't worry. We'll manage."

He hugged her back, knowing in his heart that she was right. They *would* manage.

"So what about the wedding?" he asked. "Tomorrow would be too damned far away for me, but I imagine you'll need a little time to plan things."

"Yes, but I'm well organized, remember? I could pull it all together—chapel, dress, catering, the works—in under two weeks."

He grinned. "What about the honeymoon?"

She maneuvered her hands under his coat and jacket and glided them up his back. Her fingers tripped along his spine until a shudder rippled through him.

"The honeymoon could pose something of a problem," she said. "What with your schedule and mine." She kissed his chin.

"But I want a honeymoon," he said.

"So do I. Hmm. Let's see. Maybe we should go to my apartment and start on it right now," she murmured, then she brushed her lips over his. "Just in case we can't fit one in later after we're married."

He grinned and pulled back to look at her. "No wonder I love you so much. You think of everything."

"Yeah, well, talk is cheap, *mi amor*," she said, pulling him back to her. "Why don't you shut up and kiss me?"

And he did.

THE EDITORS' CORNER

What do a cowboy, a straitlaced professor, a federal agent, and a wildlife photographer have in common? They're the sizzling men you'll meet in next month's LOVESWEPT lineup, and they're uniting with wonderful heroines for irresistible tales of passion and romance. Packed with emotion, these terrific stories are guaranteed to keep you enthralled. Enjoy!

Longtime romance favorite Karen Leabo begins the glorious BRIDES OF DESTINY series with **CALLIE'S COWBOY**, LOVESWEPT #806, a story of poignant magic, tender promises, and revealing truths. Sam Sanger had always planned to share his ranch and his future with Callie Calloway, but even in high school he understood that loving this woman might mean letting her go! When a fortune-teller hinted that her fate lay with Sam, Callie ran—afraid a life with Sam would mean sacrificing her dreams. Now, ten years later, she stops running long enough to wonder if Sam is the destiny she most desires. Displaying the style that has made her a #1 bestselling author, Karen Leabo explores the deep longings that lead us to love.

Warming hearts and tickling funny bones from start to finish, award-winner Jennifer Crusie creates her own fairy tale of love in **THE CINDERELLA DEAL**, LOVESWEPT #807. Linc Blaise needs the perfect fiancée to win his dream job, but finding a woman who'll be convincing in the charade seems impossible—until he hears Daisy Flattery charm her way out of a sticky situation! The bedazzling storyteller knows it'll be a snap playing a prim and proper lady to Linc's serious professor, but the pretense turns into a risky temptation when she discovers the vulnerable side Linc tries so hard to hide. Jennifer Crusie debuts in LOVESWEPT with an utterly charming story of opposites attracting.

Acclaimed author Laura Taylor provides a **SLIGHTLY SCANDALOUS** scenario for her memorable hero and heroine in her newest LOVE-SWEPT, #808. Trapped with a rugged stranger when a sudden storm stops an elevator between floors, Claire Duncan is shocked to feel the undeniable heat of attraction! In Tate Richmond she senses strength shadowed by a loneliness that echoes her own unspoken need. Vowing to explore the hunger that sparks between them, forced by unusual circumstances to resort to clandestine meetings, Tate draws her to him with tender ferocity. He has always placed honor above desire, kept himself safe in a world of constant peril, but once he's trusted his destiny to a woman of mystery, he can't live without her touch.

Laura Taylor packs quite a punch with this exquisite romance!

RaeAnne Thayne sets the mood with reckless passion and fierce destiny in **WILD STREAK**, LOVE-SWEPT #809. Keen Malone can't believe his ears when Meg O'Neill turns him down for a loan! Determined to make the cool beauty understand that his wildlife center is the mountain's only hope, he persuades her to tour the site. Meg can't deny the lush beauty of the land he loves, but how long can she fight the wild longing to run into his arms? RaeAnne Thayne creates a swirl of undeniable attraction in this classic romance of two strangers who discover they share the same fierce desire.

Happy reading!

With warmest wishes,

Beth de Guzman

Shauna Summers

Beth de Guzman   Shauna Summers

Senior Editor   Editor

P.S. Watch for these Bantam women's fiction titles coming in October. Praised by Amanda Quick as "an exciting find for romance readers everywhere," Elizabeth Elliott dazzles with **BETROTHED**, the much anticipated sequel to her debut novel, THE WAR-LORD. When Guy of Montague finds himself trapped in an engagement to Claudia, Baron Lonsdale's beautiful niece, his only thought is escape. But when she comes to his rescue, with the condition that he take her with him, he finds himself under her spell, willing to risk everything—even his life—to capture her heart. And don't miss **TAME THE WILD WIND** by Rosanne Bittner, the mistress of romantic frontier fiction. Half-breed Gabe Beaumont rides with a renegade Sioux band until a raid on a Wyoming stage post unites him with Faith Kelley. Together they will face their destinies and fight for their love against the shadows of their own wild hearts.

Be sure to see next month's LOVESWEPTs for a preview of these exceptional novels. And immediately following this page, preview the Bantam women's fiction titles on sale *now*!

Don't miss these extraordinary books
by your favorite Bantam authors

On sale in August:

AMANDA
by Kay Hooper

*THE MARSHAL
AND THE HEIRESS*
by Patricia Potter

TEXAS LOVER
by Adrienne deWolfe

"Amanda seethes and sizzles. A fast-paced atmospheric tale that vibrates with tension, passion, and mystery."—Catherine Coulter

AMANDA

from bestselling author
Kay Hooper
now available in paperback

When a missing heiress to a vast fortune suddenly reappears, there's good reason for suspicion. After all, others before her had claimed to be Amanda Daulton; is this poised woman the genuine article or another impostor hoping to cash in? Unlike the family patriarch, others at the Southern mansion called Glory are not so easily swayed by Amanda's claim. They have too much at stake—enough, perhaps, to commit murder. . . .

July, 1975

Thunder rolled and boomed, echoing the way it did when a storm came over the mountains on a hot night, and the wind-driven rain lashed the trees and furiously pelted the windowpanes of the big house. The nine-year-old girl shivered, her cotton nightgown soaked and clinging to her, and her slight body was stiff as she stood in the center of the dark bedroom.

"Mama—"

"Shhhh! Don't, baby, don't make any noise. Just stand there, very still, and wait for me."

They called her baby often, her mother, her father, because she'd been so difficult to conceive and was so cherished once they had her. So beloved. That was why they had named her Amanda, her father had explained, lifting her up to ride upon his broad shoulders, because she was so perfect and so worthy of their love.

She didn't feel perfect now. She felt cold and emptied out and dreadfully afraid. And the sound of her mother's voice, so thin and desperate, frightened Amanda even more. The bottom had fallen out of her world so suddenly that she was still numbly bewildered and broken, and her big gray eyes followed her mother with the piteous dread of one who had lost everything except a last fragile, unspeakably precious tie to what had been.

Whispering between rumbles of thunder, she asked, "Mama, where will we go?"

"Away, far away, baby." The only illumination in the bedroom was provided by angry nature as lightning split the stormy sky outside, and Christine Daulton used the flashes to guide her in stuffing clothes into an old canvas duffel bag. She dared not turn on any lights, and the need to hurry was so fierce it nearly strangled her.

She hadn't room for them, but she pushed her journals into the bag as well because she had to have *something* of this place to take with her, and something of her life with Brian. *Oh, dear God, Brian* . . . She raked a handful of jewelry from the box on the dresser, tasting blood because she was biting her bottom lip to keep herself from screaming. There was no time, no time, she had to get Amanda away from here.

"Wait here," she told her daughter.

"No! Mama, please—"

"Shhhh! All right, Amanda, come with me—but you have to be quiet." Moments later, down the hall in her daughter's room, Christine fumbled for more clothing and thrust it into the bulging bag. She helped the silent, trembling girl into dry clothing, faded jeans and a tee shirt. "Shoes?"

Amanda found a pair of dirty sneakers and shoved her feet into them. Her mother grasped her hand and led her from the room, both of them consciously tiptoeing. Then, at the head of the stairs, Amanda suddenly let out a moan of anguish and tried to pull her hand free. "Oh, I *can't*—"

"Shhhh," Christine warned urgently. "Amanda—"

Even whispering, Amanda's voice held a desperate intensity. "Mama, please, Mama, I have to get something—I can't leave it here, please, Mama—it'll only take a second—"

She had no idea what could be so precious to her daughter, but Christine wasn't about to drag her down the stairs in this state of wild agitation. The child was already in shock, a breath away from absolute hysteria. "All right, but hurry. And *be quiet.*"

As swift and silent as a shadow, Amanda darted back down the hallway and vanished into her bedroom. She reappeared less than a minute later, shoving something into the front pocket of her jeans. Christine didn't pause to find out what was so important that Amanda couldn't bear to leave it behind; she simply grabbed her daughter's free hand and continued down the stairs.

The grandfather clock on the landing whirred and bonged a moment before they reached it, announcing in sonorous tones that it was two A.M. The sound was too familiar to startle either of them, and they hurried on without pause. The front door was still open, as they'd left it, and Christine didn't bother to pull it shut behind them as they went through to the wide porch.

The wind had blown rain halfway over the porch to the door, and Amanda dimly heard her shoes squeak on the wet stone. Then she ducked her head against the rain and stuck close to her mother as they raced for the car parked several yards away. By the time she was sitting in the front seat watching her mother fumble with the keys, Amanda was soaked again and shivering, despite a temperature in the seventies.

The car's engine coughed to life, and its headlights stabbed through the darkness and sheeting rain to illuminate the graveled driveway. Amanda turned her head to the side as the car jolted toward the paved road, and she caught her breath when she saw a light bobbing far away between the house and the stables, as if someone was running with a flashlight. Running toward the car that, even then, turned onto the paved road and picked up speed as it left the house behind.

Quickly, Amanda turned her gaze forward again, rubbing her cold hands together, swallowing hard as sickness rose in her aching throat. "Mama? We can't come back, can we? We can't ever come back?"

The tears running down her ashen cheeks almost but not quite blinding her, Christine Daulton replied, "No, Amanda. We can't ever come back."

"One of the romance genre's finest talents."
—*Romantic Times*

From
Patricia Potter
bestselling author of *DIABLO*
comes

THE MARSHAL AND THE HEIRESS

*When U.S. Marshal Ben Masters became Sarah Ann's
guardian, he didn't know she was the lost heir to a Scottish
estate—or that her life would soon be in danger. Now,
instead of hunting down a gun-toting outlaw, he faces an
aristocratic household bitterly divided by ambition. And not
even falling in love with Sarah Ann's beautiful young
aunt could keep her from being a suspect in Ben's eyes.*

How do you tell a four-year-old girl that her mother
is dead?

U.S. Marshal Ben Masters worried over the question as he stood on the porch of Mrs. Henrietta
Culworthy's small house. Then, squaring his shoulders, he knocked. He wished he really believed he was
doing the right thing. What in God's name did a man
like him, a man who'd lived with guns and violence
for the past eight years, have to offer an orphaned
child?

Mary May believed in you. The thought raked
through his heart. He felt partially responsible for her
death. He had stirred a pot without considering the

consequences. In bringing an end to an infamous outlaw hideout, he had been oblivious to those caught in the cross fire. The fact that Mary May had been involved with the outlaws didn't assuage his conscience.

Sarah. Promise you'll take care of Sarah. He would never forget Mary May's last faltering words.

Ben rapped again on the door of the house. Mrs. Culworthy should be expecting him. She had been looking after Sarah Ann for the past three years, but now she had to return east to care for a brother. She had already postponed her trip once, agreeing to wait until Ben had wiped out the last remnants of an outlaw band and fulfilled a promise to the former renegade named Diablo.

The door opened. Mrs. Culworthy's wrinkled face appeared, sagging slightly with relief. Had she worried that he would not return? He sure as hell had thought about it. He'd thought about a lot of things, like where he might find another suitable home for Sarah Ann. But then he would never be sure she was being raised properly. By God, he owed Mary May.

"Sarah Ann?" he asked Mrs. Culworthy.

"In her room." The woman eyed him hopefully. "You *are* going to take her."

He nodded.

"What about your job?"

"I'm resigning. I used to be a lawyer. Thought I would hang up my shingle in Denver."

A smile spread across Mrs. Culworthy's face. "Thank heaven for you. I love that little girl. I would take her if I could, but—"

"I know you would," he said gently. "But she'll be safe with me." He hoped that was true. He hesitated. "She doesn't know yet, does she? About her mother?"

Mrs. Culworthy shook her head.

Just then, a small head adorned with reddish curls

and green eyes peered around the door. Excitement lit the gamin face. "Mama's here!"

Pain thrust through Ben. Of course, Sarah Ann would think her mother had arrived. Mary May had been here with him just a few weeks ago.

"Uncle Ben," the child said, "where's Mama?"

He wished Mrs. Culworthy had already told her. He was sick of being the bearer of bad news, and never more so than now.

He dropped to one knee and held out a hand to the little girl. "She's gone to heaven," Ben said.

She approached slowly, her face wrinkling in puzzlement; then she looked questioningly at Mrs. Culworthy. The woman dissolved into tears. Ben didn't know whether Sarah Ann understood what was being said, but she obviously sensed that something was very wrong. The smile disappeared and her underlip started to quiver.

Ben's heart quaked. He had guarded that battered part of him these past years, but there were no defenses high enough, or thick enough, to withstand a child's tears.

He held out his arms, not sure Sarah Ann knew him well enough to accept his comfort. But she walked into his embrace, and he hugged her, stiffly at first. Unsure. But then her need overtook his uncertainty, and his grip tightened.

"You asked me once if I were your papa," he said. "Would you like me to be?"

Sarah Ann looked up at him. "Isn't Mama coming back?"

He shook his head. "She can't, but she loved you so much she asked me to take care of you. If that's all right with you?"

Sarah Ann turned to Mrs. Culworthy. "I want to stay with you, Cully."

"You can't, Pumpkin," Mrs. Culworthy said tenderly. "I have to go east, but Mr. Masters will take good care of you. Your mother thought so, too."

"Where is heaven? Can't I go, too?"

"Someday," Ben said slowly. "And she'll be waiting for you, but right now I need you. I need someone to take care of me, too, and your mama thought we could take care of each other."

It was true, he suddenly realized. He did need someone to love. His life had been empty for so long.

Sarah Ann probably had much to offer him.

But what did he have to offer her?

Sarah Ann put her hand to his cheek. The tiny fingers were incredibly soft—softer than anything he'd ever felt—and gentle. She had lost everything, yet she was comforting him.

He hugged her close for a moment, and then he stood. Sarah Ann's hand crept into his. Trustingly. And Ben knew he would die before ever letting anything bad happen to her again.

"Adrienne deWolfe writes with power and passion."—*New York Times* bestselling author Arnette Lamb

TEXAS LOVER

by

Adrienne deWolfe

author of *TEXAS OUTLAW*

To Texas Ranger Wes Rawlins, settling a property dispute should be no trickier than peeling potatoes—even if it does involve a sheriff's cousin and a headstrong schoolmarm on opposite camps. But Wes quickly learns there's more to the matter than meets the eye. The only way to get at the truth is from the inside. So posing as a carpenter, the lawman uncovers more than he bargains for in a feisty beauty and her house full of orphans.

"Sons of thunder."

Rorie rarely resorted to such unladylike outbursts, but the strain of her predicament was wearing on her. She had privately conceded she could not face Hannibal Dukker with the same laughable lack of shooting skill she had displayed for Wes Rawlins. So, swallowing her great distaste for guns—and the people who solved their problems with them—she had forced herself to ride out to the woods early, before the children arrived for their lessons, to practice her marksmanship.

It was a good thing she had done so.

She had just fired her sixth round, her *sixth round*, for heaven's sake, and that abominable whiskey bottle still sat untouched on the top of her barrel. If she had been a fanciful woman—which she most assuredly was not—she might have imagined that impudent vessel was trying to provoke her. Why, it hadn't rattled once when her bullets whizzed by. And the long rays of morning sun had fired it a bright and frolicsome green. If there was one thing she couldn't abide, it was a frolicsome whiskey bottle.

Her mouth set in a grim line, she fished in the pocket of her pinafore for more bullets.

Thus occupied, Rorie didn't immediately notice the tremor of the earth beneath her boots. She didn't ascribe anything unusual to her nag's snorting or the way Daisy stomped her hoof and tossed her head. The beast was chronically fractious.

Soon, though, Rorie detected the sound of thrashing, as if a powerful animal were breaking through the brush around the clearing. Her heart quickened, but she tried to remain calm. After all, bears were hardly as brutish as their hunters liked to tell. And any other wild animal with sense would turn tail and run once it got wind of her human scent—not to mention a whiff of her gunpowder.

Still, it might be wise to start reloading. . . .

A bloodcurdling whoop shook her hands. She couldn't line up a single bullet with its chamber. She thought to run, but there was nowhere to hide, and Daisy was snapping too viciously to mount.

Suddenly the sun winked out of sight. A horse, a *mammoth* horse with fiery eyes and steaming nostrils, sailed toward her over the barrel. She tried to scream, but it lodged in her throat as an "eek." All she could do was stand there, jaw hanging, knees knocking, and remember the unfortunate schoolmaster, Ichabod Crane.

Only her horseman had a head.

A red head, to be exact. And he carried it above his shoulders, rather than tucked under his arm.

"God a'mighty! Miss Aurora!"

The rider reined in so hard that his gelding reared, shrilling in indignation. Her revolver slid from her fingers. She saw a peacemaker in the rider's fist, and she thought again about running.

"It's me, ma'am. Wes Rawlins," he called, then cursed as his horse wheeled and pawed.

She blinked uncertainly, still poised to flee. He didn't look like the dusty longrider who'd drunk from her well the previous afternoon. His hair was sleek and short, and his cleft chin was bare of all but morning stubble. Although he did still wear the mustache, it was the gunbelt that gave him away. She recognized the double holsters before she recognized his strong, sculpted features.

He managed to subdue his horse before it could bolt back through the trees. "Are you all right, ma'am?" He hastily dismounted, releasing his reins to ground-hitch the gelding. "Uh-oh." He peered into her face. "You aren't gonna faint or anything, are you?"

She snapped erect, mortified by the very suggestion. "Certainly not. I've never been sick a day in my life. And swooning is for invalids."

"Sissies, too," he agreed solemnly.

He ran an appreciative gaze over her hastily piled hair and down her crisply pressed pinafore to her mud-spattered boots. She felt the blood surge to her cheeks. Masking her discomfort, she planted both fists on her hips.

"*Mister* Rawlins. What on earth is the matter with you, tearing around the countryside like that? You frightened the devil out of my horse!"

"I'm real sorry, ma'am. I never meant to give

your, er, *horse* such a fright. But you see, I heard gun-shots. And since there's nothing out this way except the Boudreau homestead, I thought you might be having trouble."

"Trouble?" She felt her heart flutter. Had he heard something of Dukker's intentions?

"Well, sure. Yesterday, the way you had those children running for cover, I thought you might be expecting some." He folded his arms across his chest. "Are you?"

The directness of his question—and his gaze—was unsettling. He no longer reminded her of a lion. To-day he was a fox, slick and clever, with a dash of sly charm thrown in to confuse her. She hastily bolstered her defenses.

"Did it ever occur to you, Mr. Rawlins, that Shae might be out here shooting rabbits?"

"Nope. Never thought I'd find you here, either. Not that I mind, ma'am. Not one bit. You see, I'm the type who likes surprises. Especially pleasant ones."

She felt her face grow warmer. She wasn't used to flattery. Her husband had been too preoccupied with self-pity to spare many kind words for her in the last two years of their marriage.

"Well," she said, "I never expected to see you out here either, Mr. Rawlins."

"Call me Wes."

She forced herself to ignore his winsome smile. "In truth, sir, I never thought to see you again."

"Why's that?"

"Let's be honest, Mr. Rawlins. You are no carpen-ter."

He chuckled. She found herself wondering which had amused him more: her accusation or her refusal to use his Christian name.

"You have to give a feller a chance, Miss Aurora. You haven't even seen my handiwork yet."

"I take it you've worked on barns before?"

"Sure. Fences too. My older brothers have a ranch up near Bandera Pass. Zack raises cattle. Cord raises kids. I try to raise a little thunder now and then, but they won't let me." He winked. "That's why I had to ride south."

She felt a smile tug at her lips. She was inclined to believe a part of his story, the part about him rebelling against authority.

"You aren't gonna make me bed down again in these woods, are you, ma'am? 'Cause Two-Step is awful fond of hay."

He managed to look woeful, in spite of the impish humor lighting his eyes. She realized then just how practiced his roguery was. Wary again, she searched his gaze, trying to find some hint of the truth. Why hadn't he stayed at the hotel in town? Or worse, at the dance hall? She felt better knowing he hadn't spent his free time exploiting an unfortunate young whore, but she still worried that his reasons for sleeping alone had more to do with empty pockets than any nobility of character. What would Rawlins do if Dukker offered to hire his guns?

Maybe feeding and housing Rawlins was more prudent than driving him off. Boarding him could steer him away from Dukker's dangerous influence, and Shae could genuinely use the help on the barn.

"Very well, Mr. Rawlins. I shall withhold judgment on your carpentry skills until you've had a chance to prove yourself."

"Why, that's right kind of you, ma'am."

She felt her cheeks grow warm again. His lilting drawl had the all-too-disturbing tendency to make her feel uncertain and eighteen again.

"I suppose you'll want to ride on to the house now," she said. "It's a half-mile farther west. Shae is undoubtedly awake and can show you what to do." She inclined her head. "Good morning."

Except for a cannily raised eyebrow, he didn't budge.

Rorie fidgeted. She was unused to her dismissals going unheeded. She was especially unused to a young man regarding her as if she had just made the most delightful quip of the season.

Hoping he would go away if she ignored him, she stooped to retrieve her gun. He reached quickly to help. She was so stunned when he crouched before her, his corded thighs straining beneath the fabric of his blue jeans, that she leaped up, nearly butting her head against his. He chuckled.

"Do I make you nervous, ma'am?"

"Certainly not." Her ears burned at the lie. "Whatever makes you think that?"

"Well . . ." Still squatting, he scooped bullets out of the bluebonnets that rose like sapphire spears around her hem. "I was worried you might be trying to get rid of me again."

"I—I only thought that Shae was expecting you," she stammered, hastily backing away. There was something disconcerting—not to mention titillating—about a man's bronzed fingers snaking through the grass and darting so near to the unmentionables one wore beneath one's skirt.

"Shae's not expecting me yet, ma'am. The sun's too low in the sky." Rawlins straightened leisurely. "I figure I've got a half hour, maybe more, before I report to the barn. Just think, Miss Aurora, that gives us plenty of time to get acquainted."

On sale in September:

TAME THE WILD HEART
by Rosanne Bittner

BETROTHED
by Elizabeth Elliott